LEMNISCATE

JENNIFER MURGIA

Lands Atlantic
Publishing

Lemniscate
Published by Lands Atlantic Publishing
www.landsatlantic.com

ISBN 978-0982500583

LEMNISCATE

Chapter One

It had been raining for three days straight. I rolled onto my side to face the window towards the bit of light glowing behind the thin skin of my eyelids and grew excited for a moment, thinking today the sun might finally make an appearance. I should have known better. Under normal circumstances I would have been more than happy to cinch my covers in closer, keeping the warmth in as long as possible, thawing my flannel-wrapped arm after mercilessly sending it out into the open to slam the snooze button. But not today.

I opened my eyes to Garreth standing at the glass, his skin reflecting back a pale glimmer against the dry side of the window. My warm light on the bleakest of Monday mornings was tracing the crooked lines of water with his finger, seemingly deep in thought.

"Writing love notes to me on my window?" I mused out loud, stretching my cramped legs toward the bottom of my quilted bed. I propped myself up onto my elbow as he turned around, his striking blue eyes reminded me of his perfection.

Each day I'm astounded to find him here with me.

My angel. My guardian. My boyfriend.

Garreth has been earthbound for months now, choosing to live the life of a mortal just so he can spend each and every waking moment with me. It's not that he's giving up an extraordinary existence, he's just trading part of one for another. He's still my guardian, still here to protect me. True, there isn't anything human about him besides the charade he plays for others, and his looks, which, now that I think about it, aren't quite human either. I remember the irregular heartbeats I felt the first time we met at school last spring. The way I would feel all weak and fluttery. Words can't describe what he means to me. My mother would call it unhealthy and irrational if she ever learned the true depth of my emotions. Anyone would.

Garreth's aura isn't like the average guy running around my school or at the mall. He's pure. Surreal. And his heart beats only for me. I should feel important and flattered, I know. But honestly, it makes me uncomfortable. Why anyone would give up the freedom of roaming the heavens to be stranded here is beyond me.

Especially *for* me.

"You're awake," he said, walking slowly to my bedside. Sitting down and looking deeply into my eyes, Garreth bent to kiss me good morning. His hand rested gently on my cheek, allowing me to feel the exceptional warmth of his skin, his soft touch nearly lulling me back to sleep.

"Oh, no you don't. It's time for you to get up."

"Please tell me it's Saturday," I murmured, forcing my face into my pillow.

"Unfortunately, it's Monday and unfortunately again, we have a calculus test today." Garreth nudged my ribs and I couldn't help giggling.

"Okay, okay! I'm up!" I smiled into his chiseled face. He looked as handsome as always. His sandy hair, tousled as usual, hung seductively over his brilliant blue eyes. My eyes traced the strong bridge of his nose, which led to his perfect lips, and I let my eyes rest there for a few minutes. Picking up on my thoughts, he bent lower. I could smell the warmth of his skin, fragrant and spicy, as if he'd just showered with an amazing fragrance not yet discovered and bottled. It was *his* scent, an incense of sorts that belonged only to him and gently surrounded him like his aura. It made me dizzy, but I loved it. I closed my eyes as his lips rested softly on mine and my arms wove up and around his neck to keep him longer.

"Test? Remember?" He grasped my hands, still clasped behind his neck, and uncurled my fingers with a gentle strength, bringing them to rest at my sides. "Later . . . later you can kiss me and not let go," he whispered softly into my hair and then stood up.

"Of course *you'll* ace this test. You have infinite knowledge." I was being sarcastically playful, and Garreth rolled his eyes.

"I'll make sure I get a few wrong."

"Gee, thanks," I responded.

I could hear my mother stirring down the hall. Within minutes she'd be padding softly in this direction to her shower and stop at my door along the way, urging me to wake up.

She's not aware that I'm usually up by this point, nor is she aware that Garreth is the one to wake me before she ever gets the chance to.

A dresser drawer scraped shut, usually Garreth's clue for a silent, celestial exit, knowing twenty minutes from now he'd be knocking on the kitchen door to take me to school. I kissed him goodbye with one last chance to see the blue of his eyes sparkle like diamonds. Like clockwork, my mother's knuckles rapped at my door.

Only twenty minutes longer.

That's all I have to wait.

Twenty minutes.

Chapter Two

The aroma of singed black coffee filled the air as I stepped into the kitchen. I peered into the carafe, knowing instantly that Mom programmed the auto-start a little too early again. I shook my head and grabbed a juice and a yogurt from the fridge and leaned against the counter to chug my breakfast. My mother's heels clicked forcefully above my head, pinging loudly on the wood; stopping, retreating, then clicking faster as they inched closer down the stairs.

"Don't tell me I . . ." her shoulders slumped as she entered the kitchen, eyeing the thick goo now settling at the bottom of the carafe. The coffee maker gurgled loudly as if in pain.

"Yep. You burned the coffee again." I shot a sideways glance at the six cups of sludge.

"Good thing you're a librarian and not a barista 'cause I think Mr. Coffee is in cardiac arrest."

My mom stood staring at the coffee maker, mug in hand, as if actually considering ingesting the liquid monstrosity.

"I wouldn't if I were you," I said, scraping the spoon around the inside of my little plastic yogurt container. Mmm. Key lime.

"I'll never understand this thing," she sighed, reaching for the instruction manual.

"You're smart. You'll get it . . . eventually," I joked, pitching the yogurt container into the trash can under the sink.

She laughed and instantly, I missed her.

Mom and I had always been so close, just the two of us. My father disappeared under bizarre circumstances. I was only a baby when that happened. They had me, and then one day he just . . . disappeared. My mother never talked about it. She still doesn't. She has no idea that I know the truth about my father or the deeper mystery—the existence of my father's guardian. A dark angel named Hadrian. I had narrowly escaped his powerful influence last spring in the woods surrounding our little town. Our confrontation led to a fire that nearly killed me.

Now, life is back to normal and my mom's been spending a lot of time with the hunky doctor that bandaged me up afterwards. I'm happy she's found someone; she deserves it, and he seems to treat her well. I mean, it shows that she's happy. She dresses up more, like she's making an effort to be a person other than just my mom. She never comes home dog-tired anymore because she's so hyped up to go out later with Dr. Dean. That's his name. Dr. Nathaniel Dean, M.D. He's nice, I guess. He's a widower so I guess they have that in common. He's pleasant to me when he comes to our house, but he has to be. He's on our territory. It's just . . . I miss having her all to myself. Mom says I'm getting older. Eighteen. A senior. I should want my privacy. So maybe the M.D. after his name should mean "mom deterrent."

"Oh! I forgot to tell you; this Friday we're having our first weekly pizza party," came a muffled voice. Mom's head was in the fridge searching for lost lunch meat. I made a mental note to move it closer to the front so she wouldn't have to look so hard.

"What do you mean 'first weekly'? We've had pizza on Fridays before." I leaned down to tighten my cross trainers. Gym day. I stole a glance at the clock over the sink. Four more minutes to go until Garreth would arrive.

Mom's head emerged from around the door, lunch meat in hand. "No, I meant the four of us. You know, a weekly thing. Doesn't that sound nice?"

She turned her back on me purposefully, reaching for the bread on the far counter.

"The *four* of us?"

"Uh huh."

My mother was busying herself, avoiding the stricken look surfacing across my face.

"Did you have to ruin my *whole* week by bringing this up first thing? Now I have nothing to look forward to this weekend."

"I thought I just gave you something." Her face fell. Mine on the other hand felt permanently scowled as my grumpiness dug in deeper.

"You can still see Garreth this weekend; like you're ever apart from that boy for too long. I'm sure he'll be here in a few minutes anyway. That kid's like clockwork. "

She was attempting something she never had to do before, trying to sound strong and authoritative, and it didn't seem to fit. She knew deep down that I hated the idea.

Abhored it.

Despised it.

It was worse than catching black lung or that creepy flesh-eating disease.

One minute to go . . . way too long.

Come on Garreth. Where are you?

I looked my mother square in the eye. "Why can't the fourth person be Garreth? A nice little family dinner. Like a double date."

Mom sighed deeply, returning the stare.

"It would make us so happy if you two would just try to get along."

"She's not even his daughter!" My stress level was skyrocketing. Not a good thing for a Monday before school. I could hear my calculus grade flushing down the toilet already.

"She's his step-daughter. And it still makes her family."

"Well he's not family yet, either."

Oops. Without looking at my mom I knew I opened my mouth a little too wide with that one. I heard the refrigerator door open and the plastic salami bag slap forcefully against the back, where it would probably stay now, rotting. Then I heard the loud tapping of her shoes make their way into the small powder room in the hall.

Conversation over.

With perfect timing, Garreth appeared on the back porch, umbrella in hand, to escort me to school. I could hear the faint idling of his Jeep in the driveway.

"Hi." He leaned over to kiss my forehead, then leaned his head and shoulders into the door frame to call good morning to my mom.

"Don't bother. It's not a very good morning."

"She tried again, huh?" Garreth's eyes met mine as he noted my sullen attitude. I felt guilty this time. Well, maybe not that much.

"I guess I laid the resistance on a little too thick. You ready?" I asked, grabbing my books and my house key.

I closed the back door behind us, with my mother sulking inside. I knew things would be better when I came home this afternoon. We would eat dinner. She would try again. I wanted to make her happy, I really did, but sometimes it was hard. Dr. Dean was the first man to seriously sweep her off her feet since my father, and I had to be the one to put a glitch in things.

Garreth opened the door for me and ran around to his side, avoiding the puddles in our neglected and uneven driveway. I looked over at him and forced a smile. Being with him made me beyond happy; it was just taking a little longer this morning.

He shifted the Jeep in reverse and his warm hand found mine. I absently traced his palm with my finger, feeling the soft embedded lines that completed a circle with the intersecting points of his star. His mark never ceased to amaze me. There were days I forgot he wasn't human. It was so easy to take for granted that a person was born with human traits, little identifiable markings that showed they belonged to the human race . . . blue eyes, green eyes . . . arms and legs . . . curly hair, straight hair. And the odd little markings to distinguish one person from the other, fingerprints for example. No two were alike. Like a snowflake or birthmarks.

But when it came to the palms of our hands, I was still blown away. We were born with markings, but angels were created with their own, too. An octagram engraved in the palm of an angel's hand. It was the mark of a guardian.

I flipped his hand over, then turned mine over as well. I had my own mark. It wasn't an octagram because I wasn't a guardian, but it was just as rare and made me feel special. Garreth called it the Circle of Unity when it first appeared on my hand last spring. Circle of Unity sure sounded a lot better than what I originally thought it was, since it started off looking like an ugly, raised welt—a sure sign of some variety of poison.

I wasn't quite sure what my mark meant or why I was chosen to have it, but it didn't scare me. I've seen too much to scare easily and it was a relief knowing I'm destined for something else. Something important. Something that will never cease to exist . . . like my human life.

But human I was for now, and a stubborn one at that.

"I just wish Dr. Dean didn't come as a package deal. It really would be easier if it was just him," I said, trying to rationalize.

"You mean it would be easier for *you* if it was just him. So what you're really saying is things are difficult enough with just *one* teenager for them to deal with." Garreth smiled sideways at me, keeping his eyes fixed on the slick streets on the way to school.

"That's not what I meant." I bit down on my tongue. I was only digging myself deeper. "I know I'm no angel."

Garreth looked right at me, keeping the car steady, and raised his eyebrows inquisitively until they disappeared beneath the lengths of his sandy blonde hair.

"You know what I mean. She's trouble, that's all."

Trouble.

That didn't even begin to cover it.

I stared at the tiny drops on the windshield in front of me, not saying another word until we pulled into the student parking lot of Carver High School. It was bad enough I had to go to the same school as Brynn Hanson, but to spend every Friday now, scarfing down pepperoni and mushroom pizza with her, was pushing it.

The Jeep stopped. The rain came down heavier in large, inflated drops. Garreth made a grab for the umbrella, but I stopped him. This time I was the one to reach across and touch him. He looked at me and a warm smile formed across his lips, and then I kissed him.

"Ready to go ace calculus?" he asked, still leaning in my direction.

"Yeah, ready to fail it." I joked half-heartedly.

He rolled his eyes at me.

Miraculously, the rain was letting up a little, and by little I mean *little*. But it made me feel hopeful, not just that maybe I could make it to the front entrance without soggy sneakers, but hopeful about things in general. Reluctantly, I made a silent vow to not get too pissed off about Fridays—or Brynn for that matter.

Chapter Three

G arreth's locker was on the third level, since he was a transfer student last spring, so we split up by the main staircase and I proceeded down the hallway toward my locker, which was next to the library this year. Nothing was out of the ordinary, just a typical Monday morning: yawning students, the techno-pings of text messages being sent and received, lockers slamming in frustration. My shoes were squeaking with every step across the gray and white tiled floor, but so were everyone else's.

Then, just as my mood began to lighten, it darkened. Gone. Just like that.

It was the clicking of heels in perfect unison that penetrated my morning routine. I reluctantly turned my head to catch a glimpse of the evil foursome, quickly approaching my stretch of hallway. Lauren Atkins and Emily Lawrence were smiling, their chins held high, members of the school's royal court. Sage Fisher kept up while rummaging through her tiny handbag, pursing her glossy, pink lips together until at last, she found a stick of gum. She absentmindedly flicked the wrapper from her fingers, where it floated weightlessly to the floor. Doing my best to ignore them, I turned to my locker again. Finding my English textbook became utterly important all of a sudden.

Their leader, Brynn Hanson, was moments away from the quad where my locker stood. I stared into the cavernous metal opening and held my breath. Synchronized footsteps slowed behind me, then abruptly stopped and I sighed, having no choice but to turn and face her.

"I heard about Friday," Brynn cocked her head to one side and narrowed her eyes.

"The charity dinner?" crooned Lauren from behind us.

Brynn quickly shot her hand up, silencing her obnoxious friend. There was only one person she was giving her attention to right now.

"All I'm saying is if you're nice to me for your mom's sake don't expect any reciprocation. Come Monday morning, you'll mean nothing to me, just like any other day," she hissed through her smile.

"Don't worry, the feeling's mutual," I chided back.

Brynn shot me another meaningful glare, then looked me up and down, taking in my dressed down attire for P.E. Her eyes settled on the dampened hem of my sweatpants and her mouth turned up in disgust; then they proceeded to walk away. I could feel my face burn with anger and embarrassment.

Practically everyone was soaked from the rain this morning, everyone except Brynn, whose little leather shoes were dry and perfect. Within moments, Ryan Jameson emerged by my side, his backpack slung over his shoulder as he stared after the entourage.

"What was that all about?" he asked.

"Nothing I can't handle." I sighed heavily and slammed my locker shut.

This was a new year. My senior year. Yet I couldn't help reliving the past in these last ten seconds. It seemed like yesterday I was at my locker with Claire, my best friend in the whole world. We were approached by Brynn, who never seemed to have anything nice to say and, just before the bell rang, Ryan showed up. Ryan had been Claire's boyfriend at the time. Now, he seemed to be the only person besides Garreth who bothered to give me the time of day.

The morning bell rang, giving us three minutes to get to homeroom.

"Don't take any of her crap, Teagan," he offered. "By the way, what was she all fired up about?"

A few sophomores walking by stared at me, probably wondering why I deserved Brynn's attention. I shuddered. Any interaction with Brynn left me with a residual aftertaste that was highly unpleasant.

"My mom came up with a brainy idea. A nice, homey dinner with the very established doctor and his very demonic stepdaughter. Ugh." Hideous regurgitation sounds mockingly escaped my lips, leaving Ryan laughing.

"You're pretty funny when you're being immature," he was wiping the corners of his eyes.

"Gee, thanks."

We rounded the corner, shoving our way across the crowded hall's intersection toward our homerooms in the science wing.

"You know what I mean, Tea, and of course I think you're mature. It's just that Brynn really does bring out the best in you," his eyes were smiling behind the seriousness.

"What did you just say?"

"That . . . Brynn brings out the best in you." He hesitated, not quite sure what I was getting at.

"No, you called me 'Tea'."

"Is that okay?" I felt the nervousness rolling off of him.

Our friendship had become sort of topsy-turvy. When we first met he was the perpetually happy boyfriend of my now late best friend, but later I witnessed the cruel, destructive puppet he had become for Hadrian. Since the summer, Ryan had been on a tough road finding himself, little by little revealing snippets of the real him. Every so often, when he was willing to let his guard down, another layer would slough off. I knew deep down how hard it must be for him. To trust me. To be my friend. In a way we were both robbed by Hadrian. Robbed of ourselves. But more importantly, we share the loss of one special person. Claire.

"Besides my mom, Claire was the only other person who called me 'Tea'," I explained.

"I'm sorry. I didn't mean to remind you."

I shuffled my shoes back and forth, then looked up into Ryan's face. He looked like a puppy waiting to be reprimanded.

"No, it's okay," I instinctively reached out and rubbed his arm. "Really. Now and then things come out that remind me of her, that's all."

"Yeah," he said, still looking uncomfortable.

"Being reminded of her is okay though. I like to think of her; makes me feel like she's still here."

The light came back into his eyes and I knew I had said the right thing.

"She used to call you that all the time. You were always Tea, never Teagan, to her," he muttered reflectively. "That's just who you are to me."

A gratuitous smile slipped across my lips just as the second bell rang and then he turned and walked across the hall, disappearing through the door of his classroom. I felt a little hollow just then as I walked past the other desks to my own. A sea of questions floated in front of me. I could grab any one of them and still come up empty. What to think? What to feel? I didn't quite know at the moment.

I suppose it was a small trade. Claire for Ryan. With Claire's family moved away now, Ryan was the next best thing—the only tie left to her here. What would Claire think? A tiny part of me wanted to believe that she already knew; maybe even planned it. Ryan was the only one who knew and loved Claire as much as I did.

My thoughts shifted to my mother and the happiness I felt I was constantly blocking her from. I slumped further down in my seat, the weight of guilt holding me down like an iron grip. They had both lost someone too. Not the same person, but one of the same significance. I rolled my eyes at myself, hoping no one would catch on to the silent conversation I was having with my conscience. Was putting up with Brynn every Friday worth my mother's happiness? I sighed deeply. Of course it was.

Damn! Why couldn't Brynn be the slightest bit tolerable?

But I already knew the answer.

Because nothing ever came easy.

Nothing that was worth having anyway.

Chapter Four

"So how do you think you did?" Garreth asked, placing his hand at the small of my back as we shuffled out the door.

I drew in a deep sigh. "All right, I guess." Thank goodness calculus was over. Now I just had to sweat it out waiting for Mr. Malone to get the grades in.

We edged our way to the south hall, in the direction of my locker.

"Just for the record, it *was* a little hard," Garreth said sincerely.

"A *little* hard?" I said back, my eyebrows arched with skepticism. I knew he was joking. "Go on, admit it. The test was a piece of cake for you."

"Well . . ." he couldn't contain the smile any longer.

I leaned toward him, whispering, "And where do Guardians learn calculus?"

He leaned in, playing along with my little game, "From the great Angelic Encyclopedia."

I pulled back slightly.

"You are joking, aren't you? There's no such thing."

"Not a thing, but a who," Garreth's striking blue eyes were serious.

"And whom might that be?"

"That would be Mathur. He gives us wisdom."

"Really? Mathur?" I asked as I opened my locker, tossing my backpack and folders inside and grabbing my granola bar and Dr. Pepper from the top shelf. My stomach was beginning to rumble with hunger.

Garreth just nodded, smiling.

So many memories came flooding back to me. Mathur had been the wise elderly angel I encountered on the other side last spring. Garreth had fallen victim to Hadrian, who wanted ultimate control over humanity by corrupting our guardian angels. Without a guardian, a human is easily manipulated and vulnerable to the whims of powerful dark angels.

Without Garreth, I might have been putty in Hadrian's hands. To stop Hadrian, I needed to cross over to a realm no humans could enter. *I had to die for it.* Outwitting death with an ancient dagger inscribed with the octagram was my only hope. As it turned out, I had the power to bridge the two worlds, heaven and earth.

I took Garreth's hand gingerly in my own and flipped it over to look at his mark again, his octagram. I needed to see it, to trace it with my fingertips. I needed to know every so often that all that happened these last few months was real and not some dream.

"Maybe Mathur could give me some math pointers some day," I said, pulling myself back into the present.

"He's very wise. Like a father."

"I wouldn't know," I sighed.

"Someday you might. Your mother seems to see something in that doctor friend of hers. Maybe it's similar to what she saw in your father."

Garreth's blue eyes were tender as he leaned forward to move a strand of hair away from my face. My mom was usually a good judge of character. Maybe if I wasn't so focused on being jealous of the time she spent with Dr. Dean, the time that used to be ours . . . maybe if I wasn't so miserable thinking about Brynn and all the ways she can mess up my life inside and outside of school, I'd be able to see the bigger picture. I smiled in response to Garreth's insight.

"What would I do without you?" I leaned against my locker staring at the incredible wonder before me.

"I think the question is what would *I* do without *you?*" The space between us charged with life. He leaned into that space and placed his lips gently on mine. The hallway and the commotion slipped away in silence and there was nothing but us . . . until a Carver Crusaders' wide receiver slapped Garreth on the back.

"Hey bro, pizza and fries. The lunch of champions awaits!" Derek Arnold boomed joyously. He was a tall guy with a husky build and arms that reminded me of the old sailor cartoon, Popeye. His chestnut hair was cropped close and he was so drenched in cologne that I needed to turn away just to breathe.

Garreth's apologetic smile greeted me when I turned back around. The back of my throat tasted like Macy's cosmetic department on a Saturday.

"I completely forgot, Teagan. Derek asked me to hang out with him and the team for lunch. He mentioned it in homeroom."

"Just meet me at the truck, man," Derek gave Garreth another pounding on his back, and nodded to me, finally acknowledging my presence before bounding away. He stopped short a few lockers down to talk to a couple of freshman cheerleaders who were obviously drinking in his chokingly manly aroma and attention.

"I'm sorry." Garreth was so sincere it looked painful. "If you don't want me to go, I'll just tell the guys…"

"No, go ahead," I interrupted him. How could I be so selfish? Garreth had chosen to stay behind on earth to be with me, so we'd have the chance to be together longer than the eight days he was originally allowed. It was more than I could have ever dreamed of and here I was, keeping him to myself. Hogging him. If he wanted to look human, he should act human. He should be given more than just me; he should be given a chance to live like the eighteen-year-old boy everyone believed he was.

He looked a little lost to me. Like I had just given him permission to go hang with the wolves. I glanced over at Derek, who was tickling the underside of the chin of an overly bubbly blonde in a very short skirt. I shuddered at the display of affection.

Garreth was so not like the other guys here at Carver, but for his own sake, he had to try.

"It's okay, really. I need to get a head start on the next calc chapter. If the next test is anything like today's, I'm screwed."

"Yeah?" He was apprehensive but I could sense a little relief underneath it all. "I'll meet you here at dismissal."

Unlike last year, we only shared two classes together. I wasn't used to not seeing him during the day. I shut my locker and felt the quick kiss on my cheek. The warm feeling between us sadly disappeared, as I watched him walk away, turning back once. I smiled encouragingly and couldn't help wonder if Mathur had taught him anything else, like how to blend in with teenage wolves of the twenty-first century.

As he headed for the door at the end of the hall, I reopened my locker and tossed my calculus book and folder in a heap at the bottom. I grabbed my iPod and my keys, slammed the locker shut and headed in the opposite direction.

I started to take notice of all the people walking the halls. The guys. The girls. The Jocks, the Goths, the Bandos . . . all the cliques, all the clubs, the groups . . . the packs. I had gone to school with half these kids since kindergarten and yet I still didn't *know* them. And although Garreth had been my guardian for eight of my incarnations, I've really only known him for about five months . . . but I trusted him with all my heart.

I opened the main door to find the sun shining at last, drying up the puddle-ridden parking lot. I dodged the bigger ones still smattered here and there and made my way to Garreth's Jeep.

Using the key he had given me, I unlocked the door and slipped inside, sitting for a few moments in silence before putting in my ear buds. I closed my eyes, giving in to the tune, feeling the sun-warmed seat beneath me, smelling the scent that was his. It cleared the horrible after-smell of Derek from my nostrils and I imagined the spicy incense to be Garreth's breath, trailing down my cheeks, my neck, my arms . . . the lingering presence that constantly accompanied me, the very essence of my guardian. He was here with me.

I tried not to think of where he was, of sharing him, and instead forced myself to be happy for him.

After all, what could possibly happen in forty-five minutes?

Chapter Five

I woke with a start.

"Crap," I whispered to myself and shook my head to clear it. I looked at the blue numbers on the dashboard and sat straight up in the seat. I had slept through lunch . . . and through gym.

I stared out the window, dazed. The warm sun had only been a tease and the rain had started up again, coming down in buckets against a now blackish sky. I felt trapped in Garreth's Jeep. There was no way I could make a run for it without getting soaked, and everyone would wonder why I was so wet.

Panic settled in. *I wonder if anyone saw me?*

I needed to get inside but something in me wouldn't allow it. I couldn't put my finger on it, only there was a strong feeling telling me to stay put. Leaning back against the seat, I tried to recall what I had been dreaming about. It completely escaped me now. But there was something. I grabbed the keys from the ignition and turned around, half crawling over the seat to peer into the back.

Fabulous. No umbrella.

When the tapping came at the window, I nearly jumped out of my skin. My head crashed against the ceiling of the car as I hastily untangled my legs to turn around. I rubbed the top of my head, and cleared the inside of the fogged window with my sleeve to see out. Standing there was Garreth, drenched and expressionless. He jutted his chin, motioning for me to scoot over.

A strange, uncomfortable quiet fell between us as he climbed in and silently stared straight ahead. I couldn't read him at all. He didn't even ask why I was sitting in his car instead of at my desk in American history.

"Are you okay?" I couldn't stand it anymore. Something wasn't right.

He nodded his head up and down once, "Fine."

He didn't say anything else.

"What are you doing here?"

"What are *you* doing here?" he asked, turning to face me.

Shock and misunderstanding ran through me. I sat stunned for a moment, not sure what to say in response.

And then I smelled it.

Garreth's jacket reeked of Derek's awful cologne. The Jeep was quickly becoming saturated in the scent. The beautiful incense that had lulled me to sleep in the first place had become overpowered and replaced.

Underneath the cologne was something else. Something I realized was meant to be covered up. Each lingering moment brought it closer to the surface, each breath . . . the unmistakable smell of . . . beer.

"Were you *drinking? At lunch?*" I couldn't believe it! "Garreth?"

The look he gave me was unbearable. It was neither guilty, nor apologetic. A strange feeling came over me and I sat in silence wondering who the heck this strange boy was.

He began staring out the window and then cleared his throat, "You need to find another ride home."

"Why?"

"Because I can't take you."

"Why not?"

"Just go in, Teagan," he said, impatience building in his voice. "If you don't, they'll think you were with us and they'll give you one of these."

He held up a crumpled pink slip, then threw it on the floor at my feet. I leaned over slowly and picked it up, regarding him closely as I carefully uncurled the paper. Nervously, I read the statement printed across the center of the slip.

CONDUCT REFERRAL
REASON FOR REFERRAL:
FAILURE TO ATTEND CLASS. IMPROPER BEHAVIOR OFF AND ON CAMPUS. ACTION: 5-DAY SUSPENSION. PARENT/GUARDIAN SIGNATURE REQUIRED.

I looked up at Garreth.

"You're suspended?"

He didn't answer me.

I reread the line that stated 'Parent/Guardian signature required' and shuddered. Garreth was *my* guardian. My angelic guardian. This wasn't supposed to be happening. Who would take responsibility for him?

I hesitated, "Who's going to sign your slip?"

He reached over and took the paper from my hands, crumpling it back up. "That's my problem."

I opened my mouth, then let it snap shut.

Garreth started up the Jeep. The engine roiled, intrusive to our pained conversation. He sat looking at me impatiently, giving me my cue to leave. I studied his face, trying to find a solution to this mind-boggling predicament. Oddly, his eyes no longer sparkled. They looked more grey than blue, resembling the dampness outside the window. I reluctantly opened the passenger door and closed it behind me, standing in the rain and watching as he pulled away without so much as a glance in my direction.

When I realized how drenched my clothes were becoming I turned the other way and started across the parking lot. My legs felt heavy when I tried to step over the puddles. As I looked down to maneuver myself around them, a large black feather floated in front of me. The only witness to our argument.

It triggered something in my subconscious, but I shoved it away, braced myself against the damp chill spreading down my arms, and walked inside.

Chapter Six

My hands were trembling as I dialed.

"Hopewell Public Library; this is Diane speaking," the gentle voice came through the phone and my heart lurched. Immediate regret for my attitude at breakfast surfaced.

"Mom?" I asked into the receiver. I hated bothering her at work.

"Teagan? Is everything alright?"

Thank God she didn't still sound mad at me. There was no grudge in her voice and almost instantly my trembling hands steadied. It was my mom. The one I was missing so much these last few weeks. She would make everything better again.

"Teagan?"

"I'm here. Would you mind picking me up from school today? I don't have a ride home."

"Why isn't Garreth taking you?"

I closed my eyes at the sound of his name and swallowed hard.

"He's um . . . he went home early. Sick."

"Okay, sure. Let me get one of the volunteers to cover for me. I might be a little late, okay?"

"Okay. I'll wait in the office." I let out a huge sigh.

"I'll be there as close to 2:30 as I can get. Are *you* okay? You sound wiped out."

"Yeah, just tired. I think it's the weather." Which was true. I was sick and tired of the gloomy rain.

I ended the call, wondering what to do with myself. Maybe I could go hang out in the bathroom until study hall or hole up in one of the cubicles in the back of the library until it was time to go to the office. I did have a report coming up for English. Miss Troxell was always easy on me. Perhaps she would vouch for my absence this afternoon. My feet started walking in the direction of the library as if my mind was already made up.

I tried not to think of Garreth, but that was nearly impossible. All my thoughts were centered around him, so to *not* think of him took some serious effort, even if the voice I heard in my head now was tinged with anger. Even if the warm blue of his eyes were cloudy and hostile. I just couldn't believe he would drink on his lunch break with those idiots. My instincts were right on. They were wolves. More than anyone else, Garreth understood the power of influence. He understood temptation and being swayed in the wrong direction.

At least, I thought he did.

Was he so eager to fit in with those guys? Was he pressured? I was starting to feel guilty. He would have stayed and eaten lunch with me if I hadn't encouraged him to go with them. I shook my head, wondering how Garreth was handling this sudden turn of events.

My stomach growled and I realized that my own lunch break was sadly overdue.

I settled myself in one of the wooden cubbies in the back of the library, hoping no one would notice me. I unwrapped the now smushed granola bar and took a bite, feeling it fall like lead to the bottom of my stomach. Holding my soda can underneath the folded layers of my sweatshirt, I popped the tab, hoping the sound wasn't too obvious. It could be worse. I could've smuggled a bag of McDonald's french fries in, attracting anyone within a two-block radius.

All I wanted was to be alone.

I tried to make myself comfortable on the wooden chair and found myself wishing for the comfortable seat I had been exiled from. *I can't believe I fell asleep in the parking lot.*

Despite what happened after I woke up, there was something strange about the dream I had slipped into. The details were cloudy, but there was a balance of comfort and terror all jumbled up in it. And there was something bizarre about that feather in the parking lot.

Thirty-three minutes came and went and all I did was ponder my dream and play with the scrolled mark on my right palm. I was mesmerized, zoning in and out, making it disappear and reappear, timing how long it took. Now my hand ached from clenching it over and over and I still had a dull ache in my stomach.

After the final bell, I waited for my mother in the office, my butt numb from the library chair. I found a softer seat and stared blankly into space, chewing my bottom lip, trying to thwart off the thoughts of Garreth that played over and over in my mind. Two secretaries busied themselves behind the long formica counter, casting curious glances in my direction at regular intervals. I recognized one from last year when Garreth and I basically dismissed ourselves after my disruptive dream in history class. Garreth feared that Hadrian was closing in on us and that's when the mark on my hand came into existence.

I shut my eyes and leaned my head back against the wall, trying desperately not to think of them. Two Guardians, so alike, yet so different. But attempting to push them both to the back of my mind was futile as I tried to make sense of what just happened. And the funny thing now was that they no longer seemed so different anymore. Just unbalanced. It was adding up to something that subconsciously I didn't want to face or believe possible—that in the blink of an eye, Garreth could change.

A familiar figure strode into the office pulling me from my thoughts. My mother reached out, touched my forehead in concern and then said, "Ready?"

As we pulled away from the school, she turned up the heat in the car and eyed my damp clothing.

"What's with the wet?" she asked, returning her gaze to the street.

Without thinking it through I answered, "We had gym outside today."

"In the rain?" her forehead got all scrunchy in the middle.

"It actually stopped for a while."

Which it did.

She didn't answer.

"We started running track today."

Which we didn't.

My mom inhaled deeply and dropped the subject. Why was I lying? What was wrong with me? But I couldn't bring myself to tell her the truth about Garreth. Not yet. Maybe never.

I stared out the window, thinking how today turned out so miserably. This morning was the only nice part. The part when I woke up to find him there in my room. Now all I could recall was the far off look in his eyes in the car.

My day was crap.

And now my whole week would be equally crappy. No Garreth for the rest of the week, and Friday loomed on the horizon. Ugh. Pizza with mom's boyfriend . . . and Brynn. I could see it now, my mother playing the gracious hostess, the smiling doctor nodding in approval at her overly eager display of hospitality and Brynn . . . who would set foot in my house and butter everyone up. Probably by offering to set up a pizza topping bar or something just as equally witty, while, with each passing torturous minute, planning my demise.

Chapter Seven

After dinner I listlessly ventured upstairs, leaving my mother behind on the couch, the blue glow of the six o'clock news illuminating the living room. We had eaten with minimal conversation and I cleaned up afterward, my unspoken peace offering for this morning.

She was disappointed that I didn't want to sit with her, but with my usual excuse of homework, I trudged up the stairs with guilt in each step. Really all I wanted was to be alone and brood. I couldn't help feeling that we were growing apart with each passing day. If only I had the courage to include her in what was going on in my life, instead of keeping her at arm's length. But if I told her everything, from start to finish, including what happened over the spring and the summer up until now . . . Yeah right.

Flannel pajamas beckoned from my dresser drawer. It was only 6:20 p.m. but the day had been too miserable for words. I needed comfort. Maybe I would make hot chocolate in a little while, or tea. Tea always made me feel better.

I opened my calculus book and within minutes everything on the pages blurred together. My mind kept wandering back to Garreth. Was he okay or was he as miserable as I was? I slammed the book shut and hung my head in my hands.

The urge to call someone hit me hard. But there was no one to call. Garreth didn't have a phone. He had never needed one. I pushed the button on my computer monitor. It beeped with life. The bright glow greeted me and my fingers flew over the keys. Before I knew it, an email to Claire had been typed. Just seconds before hitting the "send" button I sat staring at the message, feeling utter loss in my bones. A tear trickled down my cheek. What would happen if I sent it? No one would answer it. Her email account was long since closed. Who else would have her email address? *MyClaire@buv.com.*

The "My" stood for the first two letters of her last name. Myers. But I always felt it was more personal than that. MyClaire. She would always be "*my Claire.*" My best friend.

My index finger hovered over the send button. I didn't need to reread the message. There was nothing written in the "subject" box. The message didn't pertain to anything in particular, just mindless babble . . . my awful day, how I missed her. I even mentioned how I'd been talking to Ryan a bit more. She would have loved his T-shirt today, a monkey with a banana up his nose. Claire loved questionable humor.

The ebb and flow of the content was more like a diary or a journal entry with no real rhyme or reason to it. I was just blowing off steam and admittedly, I felt better. For ten minutes Claire was alive to me again. I closed my eyes, hit the send button, crawled into bed and silently wished to myself that maybe somewhere, Claire would get it.

My alarm clock woke me up. Under the circumstances, I felt remarkably well. A weight of unimaginable proportion had been lifted off my chest with my spur-of-the-moment email to Claire. I smiled, imagining it had reached her on some celestial broadband. I sat up and stared out the window and felt the empty spaces fill once again.

The rain had ended, but it was cloudy and probably would be all day. Oh, well. At least my feet would be dry today. I looked around as if seeing my room for the first time. Something felt different. I heard my mother waking in the next room. If I took the time, I could calculate exactly how many minutes would pass before she was on the other side of my door.

Then it hit me.

Garreth hadn't been here to wake me.

I wrapped my arms around myself, desperately trying to recreate the feeling I had all night, the feeling of being wrapped and cradled in soft, warm arms. I even remembered words floating to me, hushed in my sleep-filled dream . . . words that had said "*I'm sorry . . . I'm here . . . forgive me . . .*" I woke with the strong feeling that Garreth had come to me in the night. That everything would be all right. He had stayed, here in my room with me. I was sure of it. I looked around, expecting him to appear, but no Garreth. No angel wings to hold me tight, yet the skin on my arms tingled as if they had just been touched. They were chilled as if I had been lying against something warm for hours.

My mother's dresser drawer scraped shut. Her feet were coming closer up the hall. I looked out into the center of my room. Nothing. I squinted my tear-filled eyes, trying to conjure an image of him, willing him to materialize in front of me just to see him disappear and be satisfied.

My jaw clenched. Panic rose in my chest.

Now. Please.

Nothing filled the space in front of my eyes.

Just the usual knock at my door as Mom's sleepy steps echoed into the bathroom.

I choked on the lump growing in my throat and numbly sat on my bed. Like in a trance, I slowly walked over to my closet and chose the first thing my hand touched to wear to school. I combed my hair into a ponytail, going through my motions without thinking or feeling anything. Before my mother even got out of the bathroom, I was downstairs making coffee. I grabbed my backpack and keys and shut the kitchen door as she was mid-sentence, calling to see if I was up yet.

My feet found their way to the alley behind our garage. My hand found its way to the lock on the door of my white Cabrio. My butt found its way to the seat on the driver's side. I started the car and headed for school, impatient to get there for once. I so desperately needed to be distracted. I needed the noise, the hustle and bustle. The gossip. The rumors. The cliques. The people I hated and didn't understand. I wanted my ears and my head to be filled with their babble so I didn't have to think of . . . him.

I parked the car and very zombie-like walked past everyone and into the school. I walked straight to the quad where my locker stood. *If Brynn comes down the hall to pester me again, I won't even look at her. If Ryan meets me here again, I won't tell him anything. I won't tell him about skipping yesterday afternoon. I won't tell him about Garreth getting suspended and what he did to deserve it. I won't tell him why my car is parked in the parking lot today instead of a gun-metal gray Jeep Wrangler. I will make it through my day just like everyone else. I hope.*

My fingers effortlessly spun the combination, the numbers flying past with experience. Right. Left. Past the zero twice. Right and slowly . . . stop on 32. The lock popped and I slid the metal lever to the right. I pulled the door toward me. A large black suede-looking feather floated out at me. The feather from the puddle. It fell to my feet, zig-zagging in slow motion, as the words from my dream came back to me.

"I'm here . . . forgive me."

My locker tilted sideways and everything was sliding. I heard buzzing in my ears as the voices of the kids around me began to fade away. They were pointing at the feather . . . wondering, laughing . . . they didn't know what it meant.

But I did.

One voice came to me. The voice from my dream. The voice that belonged to the arms and wings that held me all night, comforting me.

It didn't belong to Garreth. I was right about him not coming to my room.

An unbidden name came to my lips and I felt my mouth shaping it, making it real, rushing it out of my lungs with the breath I had been holding tightly inside my chest.

I heard the whisper with my own ears.

"Hadrian."

Chapter Eight

Amid the laughter ringing in my eardrums, I was caught by a strong pair of arms, which appeared out of nowhere before my head hit the locker. I looked up, dazed, into Ryan's concerned face.

"Are you okay, Tea?" he asked quietly, ignoring the little circle behind us that had stopped to watch the theatrics.

I nodded quickly, eager to regain my composure.

Behind us a shrill, familiar voice rang out above the muffled audience. Day two of misery had officially begun. Her footsteps clicked closer as she forced her way through the crowd and drew in an exaggerated breath of shock.

"Oh, Teagan, are you okay?" she cooed sarcastically.

"Leave her alone, Brynn," Ryan answered on my behalf. "This isn't the time or place."

"Oh, but it is. Can't you see? You're such a hero, Ryan, saving Teagan like you did. Why, did you know she's practically my step-sister?" She nodded her head as if declaring an utterly juicy tidbit to us all. I cringed at the mere idea of what the future held . . . perhaps someday being "related" to her.

"Break it up, everyone. There's nothing to see." Mr. Herman had stepped out of his classroom to break up the nosy little group that was growing in the hallway. I closed my eyes and leaned my head against the cool locker to steady myself.

"Like I said, there's nothing to see," Mr. Herman repeated for our benefit. "Be on your way, Miss Hanson."

Being dismissed was something Brynn loathed. She was supposed to be the "queen" of the senior class. As I turned to face her, she gave me a steely glare and uttered one last comment.

"Another girl falling at your feet, huh Ryan?" She did a little wave with her fingertips and added a mocking smile toward Mr. Herman as he turned his attention back to me and Ryan.

Assuming this was another student ploy to get out of class, he eyed us with suspicion. When he saw my pale, sweaty complexion his expression softened.

"Do you need to go to the nurse, Teagan?"

I shook my head, "I think I'm okay. I . . . I didn't eat any breakfast this morning."

"Mr. Jameson, why don't you escort Miss McNeel to the vending machine in the cafeteria and make sure she fills up on something decent. I'll inform your homerooms that you're present and accounted for."

"Thank you, sir," Ryan spoke for both of us.

With a nod and a concerned smile for me, Mr. Herman turned around and walked back to his own homeroom class, which by the sound of it was getting a little too comfortable without his supervision. His voice boomed, restoring order to the chaos I felt responsible for and he shut the door behind himself.

"Are you dizzy?" Ryan was still holding my elbow, afraid to let me stand on my own.

I shook my head to answer "no" and began searching the floor for the black feather. It was nowhere to be found. Who knows how many feet trampled it? But still, I looked for it, unable to take my eyes off the floor. I was so sure it still had to be here, somewhere.

"What are you looking for? Did you lose something?" We were walking toward the cafeteria for my "breakfast."

"Yeah, my mind."

I felt foolish wasting time staring at the floor, knowing we would only be excused from the short ten minutes it took to take attendance. Asking Mr. Herman to give me a hall pass to look for a lost feather from yesterday's rainstorm was not only pushing it, it was insane.

We entered the empty cafeteria, or "food court" as we sometimes liked to call it. The five vending machines standing side by side on the one wall were all we had to give variety to the masterpieces like creamed corn and Hamburger Helper. The student body liked to consider it a secret addition to the food pyramid.

Ryan deposited a dollar bill and punched the buttons A5 and E9, dispensing a chocolate chip granola bar and a yellow mini package of Lorna Doone cookies into the metal bin below. He reached in and handed them both to me.

"Here," I began fumbling with the zipper on my purse to pay him back.

"It's on me," he smiled.

"Thanks."

We walked over to one of the white laminated benches and parked ourselves as I gently tore open the package of cookies, offering one to Ryan. He shook his head no.

"So, do you want to tell me what happened back there? What did you mean by you 'lost your mind'?"

I chewed slowly, not eager to tell him *anything*. In fact, if I remembered correctly, I had just given myself a pep talk about keeping my problems to myself. That was before that stupid feather had to fall out of my locker and ruin everything. I looked at him closely, trying to read him, anticipating how he was going to react.

"You're going to think this is crazy," I warned him.

Ryan sighed and cocked his head to the side like I was stating the impossible.

"Don't you think you and I have seen enough to know nothing's crazy?" he asked.

I bit my bottom lip, wiped my mouth on the back of my hand and delved into the story I swore to myself I wouldn't tell. Before I knew it, Ryan had been given a short-but-sweet account of the dream feather coming back to haunt me, the spilling-my-guts email to his ex-now-deceased girlfriend, the too-real dream I had last night, Garreth's no-show this morning and unfortunately the whole escapade that happened yesterday; including the disgusting cologne worn by Derek

Arnold, which I made Ryan swear under oath to never wear. I also spilled the beans about Garreth's strange behavior, his drinking, his suspension and my hiding out in the library for the rest of the day.

By the time I had finished, we still had three minutes left to high-tail our butts to first period and Ryan was staring at me with his jaw hanging open.

"Gee, is that all?"

I waited for the shock to wear off.

"I mean, crap, Teagan! It all makes sense now. Wait, never mind. I don't want to go there. I can't go there right now."

"Don't worry, I'm not getting you into this," which was the absolute truth. I didn't want Ryan involved. "This is my problem." But with those words a strange trembling came over me and I felt like I had been punched in the heart. Those were Garreth's words yesterday when I asked him who was going to sign his suspension slip. It was surprisingly easy to recount every detail for Ryan. How, by talking about it, I had become strangely detached from it. But hearing those words again was like reliving it and I could hear Garreth's voice echoing in my head.

We began walking quickly back to our first period hallway when something occurred to me.

"Ryan, what did Brynn mean back there, at my locker?"

Ryan seemed to stiffen the moment I asked that seemingly innocent question. He stared straight ahead and I had to be careful to not run into any open lockers, as I kept stealing glances at his unreadable face. I followed him into the stairwell.

He still hadn't answered me. Then, he pulled my arm when we reached the bottom of the steps, yanking me back to where the storage door stood locked. He kept swallowing and looking away, either to avoid my eyes or to make sure no one was eavesdropping.

"Out with it, Ryan. What did she mean?" I was so afraid he was going to tell me something I didn't want to know.

He looked down at his feet.

"You know Brynn and her secrets. She takes a little piece of information and bends it."

He stalled for a minute, then looked at me.

"Maybe we should wait until after school," he said, shaking his head as if agreeing with himself.

"Okay, if you think that's best, but are you sure you don't want to get it off your chest now? You look like you saw a ghost or something and whatever Brynn was talking about is really bothering you."

"It's *been* bothering me for a long time now," he admitted quietly. "Getting it off my chest isn't going to take it away."

I didn't care that we were late for first period. Whatever was bothering Ryan, I promised myself I would try to understand. To help him. As far as I was concerned, all that happened in the past stays there. It was in the past. I realized at that moment that Ryan was becoming a friend I really needed right now. It wasn't like I could start over, pick someone out of the blue and go through that whole "get to know you" process. That wasn't possible anymore. Not with everything that'd happened. Too many secrets . . . and what kind of friend would that make me?

No, Ryan was perfect. We'd been through the same ordeal. We'd had the same people touch our lives. Minutes ago I opened the flood-gates and told him everything. Unconditionally, he listened. I owed it to my friend to do the same for him.

Chapter Nine

"Were you waiting long?" Ryan called out to me. He shut the door to his blue Toyota Camry and walked over, the gravel crunching beneath his tawny-colored work boots.

I stood up from the bench outside the Dunkin' Donuts and walked a few paces to meet him. I laughed, "You're the only kid I know who wears those to school. Are you the one who's been scuffing the floor?"

"Don't mess with my shit-kickers," he said playfully.

Shit-kickers? I rolled my eyes.

"Well, you know. Not *you,*" Ryan smiled.

I was right. Ryan was going to make a good friend.

"How about taking on Derek Arnold for polluting the school?"

"Gladly," he chuckled. "Bringing Derek up doesn't remind you of, you know? Him?"

He held the door open for me and I stepped inside.

"Of course it does, but I'm not going to let it ruin my life." The determination must have been strong in my voice because Ryan looked at me a little differently then. At least I thought he did. Could've been my imagination. The truth was, it *was* ruining my life. It was eating away at me and I was hating every minute of it. I loved Garreth and was worried about him. I wasn't prepared for this.

The tall pimply boy behind the counter appraised us. I remembered seeing him around school. He was quiet and his complexion needed some serious TLC.

"Um, I'll take a Bavarian cream and a medium hazelnut coffee . . . just cream, no sugar please."

"And I'll have a large black coffee and a bear claw," Ryan chimed in.

He started to dig in his pocket for money when I stopped him.

"Oh, no you don't, you sprung for breakfast. This is on me. So, speaking of not letting things ruin our lives . . ." I quickly changed the subject before he could argue with me about treating him to an after-school snack.

Ryan took the tray from the counter and followed me to a table for two in the back.

"What's ruining yours?" I asked casually.

Ryan sat quietly for a second, took a sip of his coffee, then set it down and played with the plastic flap on the lid.

"You were right about seeing a ghost," he whispered, not looking up at me.

When he did finally look up, his face showed the strangest array of emotions. I saw anxiety and fear, apprehension, disbelief. It struck me that whatever load he was carrying in his chest had been there for a while, long before Brynn's crazy statement this morning.

"You can trust me," I said, reaching out and placing my hand on top of his. No one from school was here to see us, to misconstrue this display of friendly comfort. They were all at Starbucks. Well, the pimply kid behind the counter was here, but he looked too bored to take notice.

Ryan nodded in agreement, "I know I can."

I took a bite of my donut and was all ears.

"I was driving around Sunday, just bored. I needed to get out of the house. My dad drinks sometimes. He's not the best company." He shot a look across the table to test the waters.

"Sorry, I had no idea."

"So anyway, I'm driving around and before I know it I'm driving past the cemetery. I thought I saw something and slowed down. It looked like a person walking the path, maybe visiting."

"Wasn't it pouring buckets Sunday?" I interrupted him.

"Yeah, it was. That's why I was surprised to see someone in the cemetery. I could barely see her from the road."

He took a gulp of coffee and paused. I realized his hand was shaking.

"Ryan?"

"It was her."

I could barely hear his voice, it was so low.

He looked up and I could see now that his eyes were moist.

"It was Claire."

I let out a nervous snort of disbelief and looked over at the kid behind the counter. He was stacking straws.

49

"Teagan, I swear it. It was her," Ryan leaned over, closing the space between us. The space that suddenly seemed five miles wide. He leaned toward me, reining in the distance that was suddenly huge and oppressive, as if keeping his secret from getting loose.

"What does this have to do with Brynn's comment? About girls falling at your feet? Wait. Oh. My. God."

My breath came in shallow rasps. I was having a panic attack and Ryan grabbed my arms inconspicuously, keeping hold of me.

"Listen! Listen to me!" his eyes were full of determination as he kept his grip on me.

"You were there," I breathed.

"Yes, you know I was."

"You said you were further back. You weren't near her!"

The boy behind the counter, Mr. Bored-Pimple Kid, was looking over at our table now. We were causing a scene.

Ryan hung his head. "I dared her to stand on the edge. I don't know why. The whole evening was like a dream from hell." He had tears trailing down his nose now that he didn't bother wiping.

I couldn't believe it. I wanted to call him every name in the book but couldn't quite think of the right one. Nothing seemed strong enough.

I was able to free my hands from his and leaned back against the seat, folding my arms protectively in front of me. If I wasn't too stunned to move, I would've been out of there in a second. I had been so concerned about this stupid, budding friendship between us, feeling connected to him, feeling sorry for him and all along he was an active participant in Claire's death.

I couldn't trust anyone anymore.

Finally able to find my voice, I asked Ryan the question that had been lurking beneath all the other ones.

"Did you push her?" I growled quietly.

He turned away and looked out the window, avoiding me.

Before I could say anything else, he turned back. He was a wreck as he sat shaking his head back and forth.

"I didn't push her." His voice was thick. "It was Brynn . . . but it *wasn't*."

"You're going to blame it on her because you know we already hate each other."

"I swear it's true. I don't know how to explain this to you . . ." his voice was cracking. "It's too . . . bizarre."

What a sight we must be making. The poor kid behind the counter turned his back to us now, trying to ignore the agonizing conversation we were having in his donut shop. If he was more assertive, he would have thrown us out, but with all our carrying on, it was probably best to ignore the spectacle and pretend we weren't here.

"Try," I demanded.

Ryan wiped his red-rimmed eyes.

"Brynn hates you," he began.

"Tell me something I don't already know."

"That night, after you left with Garreth . . . Brynn controlled the whole evening. Claire was convenient. She was there and Brynn knew it would hurt you. But here's the thing," he shook his head again, "this is what I can't really explain to you, and believe me, I want to tell you, I just don't know how. It was like someone else was up there on that roof with us making me listen to her and giving her some sort of control. Brynn said some weird mumbo jumbo stuff. I don't know. She was crazy that night. She kept saying it was you, but the whole time it was Claire."

Chills broke out all over my arms. I remembered my dream the night Claire died. I was Claire. I looked down at her shoes, I saw the tiny scar, I felt the wind in my face as I fell. In my dream *I* died, and I knew it before my mother came into my room with the news.

"What is it, Teagan?"

It was my turn to swallow hard and face the uncomfortable.

"That night, I had a dream about Claire falling. I saw it happen. I felt it as if it were real, but it was happening to *me*."

I shivered. Why would Hadrian make Brynn do something like that? I thought he was using humans for manipulation, not trying to kill us off.

"Do you think Brynn made your dream seem real simply by believing you were up on that roof with us?" Ryan's voice broke my thoughts.

"It doesn't make sense," I felt water logged. Heavy. Ten years must have passed since we started this conversation. "And why would you all of a sudden see Claire in the cemetery? If it really was Claire?"

"Oh, it was Claire, all right."

"How . . . ?"

"Because I was thinking about her. I was wishing I could see her again and . . ." his voice came to a screeching halt as I picked up the pieces of his sentence and finished it for him.

"And there she was."

We sat staring at each other in silence. In disbelief. How could someone wish for someone or something and get it, simply by wishing it so? That was impossible. Wasn't it? I had wished for Garreth to appear in my room this morning and that didn't happen. So much for that theory.

"You hate me," Ryan whispered.

I sat thinking. Did I?

"No, I don't hate you. I wish you could have prevented that night. But I don't hate you."

"It all happened so fast, I swear if I could've done anything . . . I wasn't myself then. You know that."

"Either was Claire," I recalled how different she had become in the course of a few days. How each of us had become forever changed by the events that happened last spring.

"Do you think it's a coincidence that I happened to be at your locker at precisely the right time this morning, right before you passed out in front of half the school?"

"Okay. Is it a coincidence?" I narrowed my eyes, unsure where we were headed with this.

"Not really. Think about it," he leaned forward again, "have you noticed me hanging around a lot lately?"

I leaned forward too. "Come to think of it, I have. What's going on?"

"I'm trying to make it up to you."

"How? By being Superman?"

Ryan exhaled a deep sigh, "Brynn's not done with you yet. I feel it in my gut. Especially since your mom is dating her dad. That's dangerous territory, Teagan."

"So what you're telling me is you feel guilty, you've become my guard dog and as always, Brynn is up to something."

He nodded.

"What's she up to?"

"Beats me, but all I know is you're already on her list and you have something she wants. I don't know what. I live with what happened every day. At least if I help you, I'll feel like I've done something good."

I let it simmer a bit. If Brynn had been willing to do me harm then . . . my shoulders slumped. Maybe she had something to do with Garreth's behavior yesterday?

That had to be it. "I think she's gotten her claws into Garreth."

"Why Garreth?" Ryan asked.

"I don't know."

Lucky for me, I was sitting across from Ryan when the light bulb went off in his head, flooding him with inspiration. A strange, happy light returned to his bloodshot eyes as he blurted out, "Your pizza dinner! It's perfect! You can start hanging out with her to try and figure her out!"

"Do I have to remind you? She *hates* me and there's no way I'm pretending she's my new BFF."

"Then you'll never know. Besides, if she does have her claws in Garreth, wouldn't you want to help him?"

I didn't answer.

"Your mom is trying to throw you two together anyway, it'll just look like you're trying to make her happy. Just be careful, something strange is going on with her. I don't know what. But based on your dream and that night, it's too weird to ignore."

Ryan took a swig of his coffee, but I just stared at mine. I always knew Brynn was trouble, I just never realized it might be more than I bargained for.

Chapter Ten

I drove by the cemetery on the way home. I didn't want to; the car just seemed to go that way, which figures. It used to be Claire's car.

The conversation with Ryan played over and over in my head. My insides felt funny.

Ryan seeing Claire really threw me for a loop. I knew she was on my mind, why else would I have written the email-to-nowhere? It was too strange that all this would surface the day after sending it. Staying mad at Ryan was hard. He could have helped Claire, but more than anyone, I understood that things were very strange that night. Just as Claire wasn't Claire, Ryan wasn't Ryan.

They were all unaware of Hadrian's existence, that he was responsible for the way they had behaved. I thought about what Ryan had said, about me being the one Brynn wanted to watch fall from the roof. God, she was going to be in my house for dinner and the girl had wanted to *kill* me?

I couldn't help wishing Brynn had been on that ledge. As much as I hated her, though, I knew that was wrong. Brynn and her friends had also been victims. Their guardians were corrupted, transforming them into twisted humans who no longer knew right from wrong. But things didn't go as planned. I shuddered at the thought. Thankfully, Garreth showed up in time to help me. *Garreth.* I let out a big sigh, and started to wonder if maybe Brynn's guardian was still corrupted.

I pulled into the cemetery past the black iron gate held open during "visiting hours" by a thick tattered rope. Claire's car trailed around the winding loops, past the little shed that stored God knows what and up the incline toward her grave. I never went to her funeral. I couldn't bear it. I had only visited her grave in a dream and it wasn't pretty. It certainly wasn't the way I wanted to remember her.

Sloping around the bend of Japanese maples, I let the car come to a stop and idle. I was tempted to get out and walk through the sodden grass to look for her marker, but I stayed put. It felt colder here. As I reached to turn the heat up something out of the corner of my eye caught my attention.

Piles of leaves had been raked, ready to be bagged and taken away. They looked darker than usual, soggy and wet from the never-ending rain we'd been having. Pressing my nose up to the glass for a closer look I tried to make out the colors. The once brilliant foliage was now faded and grayed, reduced to muck. They barely stood out against the crunchy-turned-mushy brown and black . . . wait. Why were there black leaves? Then I realized they weren't *all* leaves. Raked up among the rot were black feathers. I squinted and rubbed my hand across the glass, wiping clean the condensation from my breath.

They were poking out randomly, the black down was clumped, held together by thick quills. Like the feather from the puddle. Like the feather from my locker this morning. There were so many, as if a raven had gotten into a vicious fight with another animal and lost. But there were too many feathers for one bird to lose.

Unless, the bird was huge.

Unless, the bird was the size of a man.

An icy chill spread down my arms and I pulled away from the window. Suddenly I was freezing cold. I cranked the heat dial up to the highest setting but the warmth from the vents wasn't going deep enough to kill the chill. I drew in a deep breath, closed my eyes for a second and then laughed nervously as I reopened them.

"You're losing it, Tea," I muttered to myself uneasily, staring out at the piles once again. Feathers poked out in several spots, but not nearly as many as before. I grabbed the steering wheel and squeezed hard, trying to convince myself it was all in my head. But I found myself putting the car in drive. I was getting out of here.

I turned the wheel and stepped on the gas, backtracking around the looping, narrow path and ignoring all the ten mile per hour signs. The main road was just up ahead.

My body was shaking with a cold sweat by the time my little white car passed through the gate. Instantly, I was jolted back to the one dream I wanted to forget—my dream visit in the cemetery. Everyone had left Claire's funeral, but I wasn't alone. There had been an enormous creepy raven hovering nearby.

Suddenly I felt eyes watching me from behind, I stepped on the gas and without looking back tore through the streets of Hopewell until I reached home.

I opened the back door to a dark and empty house and flicked on the kitchen light. A note from my mom was waiting on the counter.

Out with Nate. Food in fridge. Love, Mom

Good, I thought to myself. At least I didn't have to explain my shaky emotional state. I was such a wreck she was sure to think I robbed a bank or was doing drugs or something. I tried to calm myself, replaying what had happened. I freaked out at a pile of leaves in a cemetery. That's all they were. Just leaves. I kept telling myself that and tried to settle my nerves.

I wasn't hungry, but instead, felt a little crampy. I checked the calendar. *Yeesh. Twenty-eight days already?* I headed up for a nice warm shower to ease the lingering chill, flicking on every light switch along the way.

The warm water streamed down my skin but I was still shivering. If the shower had been any hotter my skin would have burned. I leaned my forehead against the tiled wall, feeling the water soak my hair and trickle down my nose where it plunked to my feet. It didn't help. I turned the water off and wrapped myself in a soft towel.

Plodding to my room, I got into my pajamas and sat on the end of my bed, feeling both tense and strangely empty.

The after effects of Hadrian should be long gone by now. In fact, most of the kids in school were acting completely normal. The ones who had suddenly looked empty, showing that their guardians had been taken, were fine now. I remembered the way the air would grow chilly whenever their guardians were ripped away. That wasn't happening now. Things seemed back to normal. Well, except for Brynn. But maybe she never even had a guardian.

I thought of Garreth.

No, things weren't normal.

Things sucked.

I flopped back on my bed, my wet red hair falling in chunky tangles, as I hadn't bothered to comb it. I curled up tightly on my side, pulling my quilt up to cover my legs. I felt cold and sick and empty.

Was it possible this was all my fault? Did he stay here too long? Long enough to make him act and feel like a real human? Maybe this was a really bad side effect of being earthbound. But isn't that what I wanted for him when I watched him follow Derek down the hall? This must be why he's mad at me. I caused this.

I tucked the quilt beneath my head. My covers were getting wet from my hair, making me cold all over again. I tried to stay focused on Garreth, but other thoughts wormed their way in. I needed to figure this out, not only to help him but also to keep myself from losing my mind. But my mind strayed to places it didn't belong.

Sleep was coming for me. I was floating in myself as the fear I felt inside seeped away. I thought of black feathers and wings . . .

I willed Garreth's face to appear in my mind, but his face changed to another . . . one with dark hair, pale skin, green eyes . . .

I felt a crushing sensation in my chest.

And I felt miserably guilty.

Chapter Eleven

"Wake up, Teagan. School," my mother called from the hallway.

Without Garreth, I was totally unprepared for her morning knock at my door. I refused to start the day feeling empty, so I refocused. Stretching my arms and legs as far as they would allow, I remembered it was Wednesday and in two days I would be sitting down to dinner with Brynn and Nate.

Hmmm. Maybe Ryan's right. Maybe there is a way to find out what she's up to.

"I'm up," I answered back, hearing my mom close the bathroom door.

Surprisingly, I had slept fairly well. I didn't ache so much and no longer felt chilled. I lifted my hand to the top of my head and felt the chaos. I had forgotten about my hair and would have to spend extra time this morning trying to tame it.

I sat up and looked around. My room was the same as always. I wasn't expecting any company this morning so I flipped the covers back, ready to swing my legs over the side of my bed.

Then I saw it. It had been next to me all night, under my covers.

I picked it up and looked around, but there was nothing, not even in the corners where the shadows fell silently.

I took the feather between my fingers. It was so long that the ends brushed my lips. I closed my eyes, thinking of him. Then, I took the sharp end of the quill and very lightly, pricked the inside of my arm. I opened my eyes to see a dot of red expand from the tiny puncture and swell like a crimson bead on my skin.

I drew a shaky breath into my throat.

If I closed my eyes again, I would see it, the picture of us. The one that refused to go away.

. . . his wings beating wildly, lifting us up off the stone floor of the chamber . . . the loose quills piercing the tender flesh of my arms as he held me close to him and then the delicious sensation of his lips pressed against my skin, kissing away the pain . . .

Quickly, I grabbed a tissue from my nightstand and dabbed my arm, holding it down a few seconds to stop the bleeding. I looked around, feeling paranoid.

I don't believe I just did that.

One-handedly, I made my bed the best I could, tucking the feather into the underside of my pillowcase. In a flash I got dressed, spritzed the unruly mop on my head with the water bottle I kept on my dresser and bounded down the steps, remembering to eat breakfast. For some reason, I couldn't help the smile from creeping onto my face. I tried to put a finger on my feelings. Was I happy? I was still nervous. I mean, a feather managed to get stuck underneath my pillow sometime during the night. How normal was that? But I felt safer now, to a degree.

Even if the feather was black.

And the feeling stayed with me all the way to school. My classes came and went without incident. Nothing fell out of my locker except the usual calculus book, which I kicked every time it jumped out at me. I saw Ryan before homeroom and then again before lunch and both times he appeared apprehensive. He probably thought that overnight, rationality had permeated my senses, making me realize that I really did hate him. Even with my reassurance, he didn't seem too convinced.

It didn't help that by the end of the day, my cramps were killing me and I was positive Ryan thought my sudden withdrawal had something to do with him. How do you explain cramps to a guy? I knew the answer to that one. You don't. Instead, I made my way to the third floor bathroom.

I was just about to grab my purse from the metal hook on the last stall door when a small group of girls strolled in. I recognized their voices immediately. Peeking through the little, narrow opening by the door, I had a sideways view of Sage and Lauren. They were at the mirror, primping, obviously in love with themselves. Emily was leaning down, and from what I could tell, she was rolling a miniature lint roller up and down her expensive black tights. I realized then that Brynn was not with them and I strained my vision, pressing my face right up to the door in case she was further away out of range. Not only were they without Brynn, but the absent leader of their hateful little group was also the topic of their discussion.

"What is her obsession with that girl?" Lauren's squeaky voice filled the tiled room.

"Beats me."

It was Sage who answered her, her gold bracelets jingled as she held her arm up, looking for signs of white beneath her brown, toned arms.

Who would wear a tank top in fall?

As I eavesdropped, it amazed me how superficial their group really was. Not that I thought any of them held any depth or consideration, but it dawned on me how tactless they truly were. *To each other.* They were bashing Brynn as if she were an outsider, which shocked me. I thought their type stuck together. But as they recounted Brynn's personal business, I realized they were also talking about me.

Emily chimed in then, tucking her trusty little lint roller back into her bag, "I know, all she does is talk about how she's going to ruin the girl's life. I mean, come on! Why bother!"

"Hello? Her dad is dating her mother. That practically makes them sisters."

"Eew."

I pressed my ear to the opening but they were walking further away from the mirror.

"Well, whatever she's planning to do, I hope she gets on with it. She's acting weird."

"Yeah, I like wearing black and all, but . . . save it for the runway." Lauren let her sentence trail off as soon as the lip gloss applicator touched her already perfect mouth. "What's with that book she keeps looking for? The one in her dad's library?"

"Who cares! I say this Friday we go to that party without her. I mean, she's got some little dinner to go to anyway, doesn't she?" Sage was clearly annoyed. "I'm not ruining another good party at Marc Slater's just so Brynn can play scavenger hunt through her dad's dusty old medical books. I heard Marc found his dad's stash of rum!"

"You're right, but do you think he put her up to it?" Lauren asked as they filed out.

Just like that, they were gone and I was left alone in the bathroom shaking.

Black? Raiding her dad's office? What was Brynn getting into?

I didn't like the sound of this and obviously her friends were getting bored of Brynn's idea of weekend fun. Luckily, they were all too shallow to read into what this could really be about. Something was not right with this. I knew Brynn hated me but after Ryan's warning that she was still after me, and the revelation that it was supposed to be me on the roof at the rave last year instead of Claire . . .

If ever there was a time I needed Garreth to calm my nerves, it was now. But he was absent in more ways than one. I took a deep breath and stepped out into the florescent glow of the bathroom. I splashed some cold water on my face, dried it with a paper towel, and walked quickly to my locker, grabbing everything I would need. The walk to my car took longer than usual. Each step felt like a step backwards as I thought of the impending weekend.

As soon as I got home, I was promptly shuffled from my car into my mother's Honda. Together we drove to the store for pizza supplies for Friday night.

I followed her around, aimlessly pushing the metal cart like an eight year-old. When you're eight it is a big deal to push the cart up and down the aisles. It isn't when you're eighteen and a senior and the little gray-haired ladies still smile at you as if you're the biggest help in the world.

My mind wandered, as usual, and I tried to steer it towards matters of importance—like the calculus homework I had to tackle or what conditioner to buy so my hair never looked the way it did today again. Ever. Then the inevitable happened and my mother dropped a series of bombs. As hard as it was to swallow, the first one was expected. In fact, I expected it yesterday, but I guess she was just trying to be nice.

We were in the frozen food aisle when she asked, "So how is Garreth doing? He hasn't been around lately?"

"He's just not feeling himself," I said quietly. It wasn't a lie. Our last conversation, the one I'd been avoiding, played through my head. He definitely didn't act or sound like himself.

"Hmm. That's too bad. Let's stop over at the spice aisle. Brynn came up with the idea of having a topping bar! How brilliant is that?"

I rolled my eyes.

The next ten minutes were taken up by intense decision making. Parmesan or parmesan-romano? Crushed peppers or creole powder? Garlic powder? Garlic salt? Garlic flakes? By the time my mom made the earth-shattering choice of what we were all going to shake onto our pizza, I had spaced so severely that I may have even drooled on myself.

Thankfully, the toppings were the last thing on the list. As we were checking out, Mom asked if I wanted a magazine or a candy bar, just like she used to when I was little. After picking out a pack of gum, I noticed she looked a little antsy all of a sudden, like she couldn't wait to leave. Well, geez, she could've felt that way back in the spice aisle.

After paying we walked to the car and she carefully placed the bags in the trunk. I realized that she wasn't being cautious for the groceries' sake but for mine as she turned to me and half-whispered "Nate's asked us to move in with them."

I stood staring at her like an idiot, unable to move. Really.

"Honey? Well, what do you think?" she was giving me one of her strained smiles. The kind where it's sort of painted on her face and overly cheerful. But it was starting to crack from the tension.

Without a word I turned, opened the passenger door and got inside, shutting the door on the mess that had just exploded in my face. I didn't have to look out the window to know that my mom was still standing there, dumbfounded. I could visualize her biting the inside of her cheek, the crease forming deeply on her forehead. I heard her mutter "alrighty then," and then she got in on her side and we drove home in complete, uncomfortable silence.

Chapter Twelve

Silently, we unloaded the groceries and then went our separate ways for the rest of the night. Guilt consumed me as I tried to focus on equations and found myself padding inconspicuously into her bedroom, waiting by the doorframe for her to notice and invite me in.

She looked tired as she peered over the top of the novel she was reading. Again, the guilt pangs hit me hard as I realized something. Our disagreements seemed to wear on her, but when she was with Dr. Dean she looked years younger. When she talked about Dr. Dean she gushed like a teenager, going on and on like a first crush, stopping only when my ears rang painfully and I couldn't take it anymore.

I shook my head and stepped into her room. She patted the covers next to her and I quietly climbed in beside her, curling up on my side.

"Homework done?"

"No," I answered, letting that subject drop. I took a deep breath then asked, "Do you really love him?"

She slid her finger between the pages she was reading and let the book rest on her chest. "Can you believe it? I really do."

"Why?"

She looked away thoughtfully, then sighed and her gaze rested back on me.

"For a long time I've been the happiest person in the world," she smiled.

I was confused. I thought living with me was difficult, but then remembered it's only been that way recently. "You are my life, Teagan. Losing your father was hard, but it was you who helped me through it. You do realize you saved me? If I didn't have you, who knows what kind of person I would be right now."

This wasn't the first time I had heard this story. How the responsibility of taking care of me had kept her grounded. I was also her one last link to my father. Wasn't it painful that I reminded her of him? I knew she loved me, but I still couldn't help feeling guilty. Now I understood my need to reverse the roles . . . why I wanted to take care of her. I've been feeling responsible for her well being all along.

"But . . . sorry, that doesn't really answer my question."

She cupped her hand beneath my chin and looked at me thoughtfully.

"When I met Nate in the hospital with you, I was so grateful to him . . . but there was something else there. A connection. I know it sounds silly."

"No it doesn't, go on," I urged.

For a fleeting moment I felt like we were two girlfriends, having a sleepover and gossiping about guys.

"When I looked at him to take his card," she blushed. "I was reminded of how it felt when I met your dad. He makes me feel like me again, and she's someone I've missed for a very long time."

I smiled up at her. How could I take this away from her? She was so happy with him.

"He's a good guy, Teagan. He doesn't have to be your *father*. Just give him a chance to be your friend."

"I'm sorry I've been such a pain, Mom. I know he makes you happy. It's just . . ." I let out a huge sigh. "You know Brynn and I don't exactly get along, so she gets in the way of my getting to know him better."

"She's no cup of tea, that's for sure. Even Nate has issues with her."

"Are we moving in with them?" I buried my head beneath her arm, afraid of the answer.

"I'd love to, but no, I'm not going to ask you to move."

"But . . . then why?" I stammered, bringing my head up to look at her.

"I was just trying to have a heart-to-heart conversation with you, sweetie. Don't you realize that I've missed the way we used to talk to each other?"

I nodded sheepishly, "I miss it too."

"Do you know how long it would take to list this house and pack all our junk up? This house probably wouldn't even budge on the market until after your graduation."

I giggled nervously, realizing my overreaction.

"Did you think we were going to move in this weekend?" she asked.

"If we ever do move in with them, just put me on the opposite side of the house. Better yet, a different floor."

"She can't be all that bad." She smiled, shaking her head.

"Don't even go there, Mom. She's evil."

"Nate thinks it's the friends she hangs out with, that they're a bad influence. He's sort of an expert on all that."

"What do you mean?" I asked, curling up under the covers.

"Oh, he's a brilliant man. He has all sorts of theories and ideas on humanity and ethics. Why people are the way they are. It's amazing he chose the medical field. He could have easily gone into philosophy or history. You know, he even has a theory about that funny scar on your hand."

My ears perked up the moment the words came to her lips and I clutched my right hand tightly beneath the covers. Only a few, select people knew the truth about my scar. It was pure luck that the fire in the woods burned my hand, camouflaging my mark.

"So, what's his theory?" I tried to keep my voice steady.

"Just that it looked a little unusual for a scar. He said it actually looks like an ancient brand."

I raised my eyebrows. "Brand? As in ownership of live-stock?"

My mom let out a laugh, "Yeah, I guess so. He said it was similar to a mark of protection he researched years ago, but it's just coincidence. He said maybe the heavens branded you for protection from the fire, and that's why you were given the strength to not only survive it yourself, but to save Garreth as well. It's kind of a nice thought when you think about it. You were both very lucky that night."

I tried not to think about that night, when I thought Garreth was lost for good. It had seemed his time here on earth, eight amazingly short days, was up. But even though my guardian stayed earthbound, it seemed he was still lost.

Oblivious to my sudden silence, my mother kept on talking about Dr. Dean and his "theories" and how he thought there were answers to everything and everyone; like a blueprint mapped out for everyone since the beginning of time, and how my mom thought he was an amazingly deep man.

"He keeps every theory logged so he can refer back to it if he needs to. He's so organized," my mom continued.

"What do you mean 'logged'?"

"Oh, he writes all his thoughts down in a journal."

"Sort of like a diary? Isn't he a little old for that?" I was beginning to yawn and it occurred to me that my homework was still sitting on my desk and it wasn't getting done by itself.

"It's more like a record book, with actual dates and times. Real-life accounts for strange phenomena. He's been keeping the journal forever and it's kind of battered and old looking. Hey, that's a great idea for a Christmas present for him. Don't let me forget that one."

Bits and pieces of the conversation I had overheard in the bathroom at school came floating back to me and I wondered, could the book Brynn's friends said she was hunting for be the very same journal my mother was describing? If it was in fact one and the same and Dr. Dean had some crazy notions about my scar, then I certainly would be an entry in that journal. Wouldn't Brynn just love to get her hands on any information she could use against me? Especially if that information was surreal.

But what would Dr. Dean want with information like that? Was he just a studious adult nerd that liked to keep track of strange subject material? And what were the odds that his step-daughter was Brynn Hanson, of all people. It seemed too strange to be a coincidence.

There was something else, something I had overheard in the bathroom.

Shoot! What was it?

I wracked my brain for it to come back to me. It was just a snippet that didn't mean anything . . . at least not until now anyway.

Then I remembered.

"Do you think he put her up to it?"

Who was "*he*"?

As the subject we were just on blended into a new one, I excused myself, responsibly saying I had homework to finish up. But before leaving her room, I lingered in the doorway.

"Mom?"

"Hmm?"

"Do you believe in guardian angels?" I asked warily.

A sweet, reflective smile appeared across her face.

"Of course I do, honey."

I returned her smile and went to my room.

I felt the overwhelming need to talk to Ryan just then. He was the only person right now who I could talk to about this, the only one who understood how Brynn despised me. He knew how twisted and sick she really was, and the lengths she would go to get what she wanted.

My head was dizzy from thinking.

Brynn, Dr. Dean, my mother . . . how did this all connect?

An unsettling feeling washed over me. Whatever this puzzle was, it couldn't be good.

Oh Garreth, I need you.

He was supposed to protect me but where was he? Suspended for underage drinking during lunch hour. Of all the idiotic things. I felt tight, scalding tears form in the back of my throat. I had no idea what to do about Garreth but if it came down to me helping him again, then yes, I would help him.

I looked at my hand and willed my mark to appear full and strong on my palm. I was so confused. Was I to be the one to save my guardian from here on out? Was I the stronger one now? I didn't feel very strong. I felt lonely and hurt and confused. Then to make matters worse, let's just throw Hadrian back into the mix. I was seriously beginning to think he was haunting me, with the feathers and all. I mean, face it. I'm a magnet for chaos. I had my doubts that had anything to do with Brynn unless she was striving to make me insane. Which, I suppose, did sound like her. No, face it. I was good at attracting the weird and unexplained and keeping it close at hand. Why couldn't I just be normal?

I tried to cast aside my confusion and paranoia. Right now I had to focus on the task at hand.

Right now I needed to get my hands on that journal.

Chapter Thirteen

Sleep had not come easily.

In fact, it was hours before my body finally melted down and gave up. But even then it wasn't restful. It was garish and unpleasant, full of strange dreams and even stranger faces. I felt like an unseen ghost, a whisper of someone else's thoughts traveling through someone else's nightmare.

Sitting up, I placed my hands over my eyes to filter out the light billowing in through my window. My sensitive eyes blinked painfully as the blinding yellow glow made a beeline for my sleep deprived head. Then I remembered, I needed to talk to Ryan today. But wading through the six hours of school would be torture, not that it wasn't when I *didn't* have something important on the threshold. But this, the waiting to talk to him, to tell him about the strange, old book and Dr. Dean's hobby—this might get us somewhere and the closer we got to stopping whatever Brynn was up to, the better.

I couldn't even begin to wrap my head around whatever Brynn was planning. I honestly thought I had been through it all after dealing with a dark angel last year. It seemed that Brynn and Hadrian had traded places this year. Now I was more concerned about a high-heeled, cheerleading menace than a malicious archangel.

There was no way I could stand waiting until after school to tell Ryan about Brynn and the book or my plan for us to sneak into Dr. Dean's house tomorrow night and search for it.

Complaining to myself was only making matters worse. I needed to vent. As the overwhelming need to get things off my chest became more unbearable, a thought came to me. A soothing little piece of reassurance. Despite the few minutes left before I needed to get downstairs, I seemed to float effortlessly over to my computer. There was someone who would hear me out and not judge or look at me sideways. Someone who would just plain listen.

I drummed up the nerve before the fleeting moment of inspiration left me. Why not email Claire again? It had made me feel a million times better the other day and besides, who's going to tap into the closed email account of a dead person?

No one, that's who.

The deep breath I took filled me with confidence and once again my fingers flew across the keys, my heart and soul pouring out through their tips like never before. I had written to Claire the other night, but it wasn't like this. Today there seemed to be a silent desperation within me that was lacking in the previous email. Finally, all the emotions I had stored up inside over her absence, her death, seemed to have boiled over, and now there was no stopping it. In my mind, I could picture Claire so clearly, as if she were in the room with me and because of this, the words flowed effortlessly.

I recounted the ever-growing personality change in Brynn. That, paired with the existence of a peculiar journal that has now lead to suspicions about the man my mother was dating, was more than I could keep to myself. I had been reluctant to pull Ryan into the discussion but it felt right, so I revealed my daring plan (the one he didn't know about yet). I only paused once to briefly question my hesitation about the plans with Ryan. I realized this made them more real. Solid. And now that I had told someone, now that I had told Claire, there was no backing out.

My fingers continued at the keys with driving determination. The dam had broken. I admitted that my feelings were being stretched thin between Garreth and Hadrian, and how I wished with all my heart she were able to answer me somehow. I would do anything to see her roll her eyes at my dilemmas, to give me the sound advice only she was capable of giving.

Glancing at the clock, I realized I needed to wrap things up. In closing I asked Claire to forgive me for not being a better friend. I knew deep down that I should have stayed at the rave with her and yes, maybe I would be dead instead of her, or maybe we both would have lived. Who knows.

My finger touched the send button and in a flash the lengthy note I had just typed disappeared and was swept away into the universe, taking a chunk of my pain with it.

Chapter Fourteen

"Are you serious?" Ryan's face paled at my idea.

"It's exactly what you said we should do," I insisted. "Well, not in those exact words, but you did say we needed to find out what Brynn was up to. You have to admit, she may not be the only one in her family with strange habits these days."

"Yeah, the whole journal thing doesn't sit well with me either," Ryan agreed, rubbing his chin with his hand in a very philosophical way. "How are we going to get Brynn out of her own house again?"

"We're not, she won't even be there."

I proceeded to spill the details of my plan and after hearing my own voice say it out loud, I had to admit it sounded very Nancy Drew of me. I could see Ryan thinking it through, but his eyes still seemed a bit wary, which was only natural. My own insides were nervous. For one, I needed to create a diversion, somehow letting Brynn know about the party her friends were going to. Then, we needed to break into the doctor's house, while he's at my house getting it on with my mom.

Eew, bad mental picture.

I kept telling myself that this was the only way. Why would my mom's boyfriend, an established doctor, keep a creepy journal about strange phenomenon? Why would he even have any theories about me and my scar in the first place? I didn't trust him. Not last month, not last week and especially not now, and I especially didn't trust Brynn, the evil stepchild.

I left Ryan at his locker quad, agreeing to meet under the tree at the end of my street tomorrow night. We were going to get to the bottom of this, I felt sure of it.

All of a sudden, my hand blazed so intensely, I had to cup it in my opposite hand. It was usually a warning when it felt like this, and so I began searching the groups of kids still lingering in the hallway with me. My ears listened intently for wings, thinking perhaps this was a strange reoccurrence of the black feather incident.

I craned my neck, trying to peer into the vast crowd near the stairwell doors. My legs suddenly felt rubbery and jellylike. I couldn't tear my eyes away from the back of a very familiar head that unexpectedly turned. He walked straight toward me, causing everyone in his path to stop and stare. He wasn't supposed to be here. We all knew that. Like any other high school, word travels quickly. People were whispering, but he seemed to float effortlessly past them. Keeping his stride, he seemed to have a hidden agenda, pausing only for a second to glance at me with his deep blue eyes. Then he looked straight ahead and kept walking.

"Whoa, did you see that?" someone's voice broke the stillness around me.

"I thought he was suspended," someone else whispered a few lockers down.

The air felt stifling and I had to get out of here. I needed air.

What did I do wrong?

Breaking through the groups scattered throughout the hallway, I pushed past anyone in my path, ignoring the rude comments left behind in my wake. I walked past Mr. Herman as he bent down, propping his door open with a worn wooden wedge, nearly stubbing my foot on his hand. He said something that sounded like my name and some reference to turning back around . . . I ignored him. I ignored them all and flung my arms out in front of me, pushing the glass double doors out of my way.

I walked to my car, never breaking my stride. With peeling rubber, I backed my little white car out of the parking space, put it in gear and drove beyond the school grounds, never looking back.

My mind replayed that day in the parking lot over and over again and still, I had no idea what I did to deserve this pain he was putting me through. He was the one who messed up, I kept reminding myself. He was the one. Not me.

Then why was he punishing me?

I didn't stop until I reached the bend in the road. Autumn ravaged remains of green and gold flitted wildly past the sides of my car as I sped up the too-narrow pathway, now resembling an overgrown driveway. I lurched forward as my car came to a stop and I closed my eyes, willing the burning hot tears to stay put as I leaned my forehead against the hard steering wheel.

The world was still. Total silence. No birds. No rustling of leaves or branches. I opened my eyes and drank in the barren void surrounding me. Slowly getting out of the car, I stepped out onto the soft carpet of pine needles and ground mulch. Everything was brown and still. Charred stumps of trees flanked the desolate clearing as wild fern wilted with brown bending leaves scattered the ground.

It had been months since I was last here. Garreth and I had come back the day after the fire. It still held a feeling of magic that seeped through the ruin, still held the promise of new life rising from the ashes – but all I could see around me now was devastation.

Blackened bark curled and clung to the fragile trees that still stood, though the wooden trunks were dehydrated and petrified inside now. Practically everything here had died that night. I blinked and looked around, feeling heavy and lost, but I couldn't will myself to turn around, get back into my car and drive away. I too felt hollow and burnt and tried to will my feet to leave this place but couldn't. I belonged.

I turned to face the old chapel foundation that still stood here. My legs managed their way over the cracked twigs and gnarled roots of long dead trees. I stumbled past the long fallen tree Garreth and I had once used as a bench, now blackened and splintering. My feet stopped at the bottom of crumbled rock, steps that now led to a ravaged opening to nowhere. The chapel. I remembered her beauty. The stained glass triangles of color that had glinted in the sun were now broken and pulverized into glittering sand. The arched wooden door was missing and rusted metal hinges nailed to crumbling mortar was the only welcome. I carefully stepped up and stood in the doorway, feeling the painful loss of this place. Feeling its misery.

The red candles had all melted and bled across the floor in the fire. The altar where Garreth had revealed his true self to me had crumbled like the walls, which were no higher than my knees.

Sadly, I looked up at the large opening in the trees that resembled a gaping mouth. The flames had not reached that far. I closed my eyes, remembering the tower that once stood here, though I had only seen it once. I had come running to this place when I died, wild and frantic to save Garreth. Giving my life for his was easy. I would still give it if he were to ask.

And no matter how rotten things were now, I had to believe there was a solution.

I held my hand up in front of my face and studied the lines of my special mark, hopefully for the last time, then before I could change my mind, I made it disappear.

I was so lost in myself, I almost didn't hear it.

The movement. The rustling.

That's when I felt it.

Eyes staring at me.

I pivoted quickly on my heels and stared at the trees surrounding me. The coldness that swept across my arms pulled me out of my depression. I wasn't alone and whatever was in these woods wasn't friendly.

My hand went numb just then and when I pulled it up to look at it, my mark had reappeared.

Wasting no time, I hurried back to the car, slammed the door and high-tailed it out of there. I drove backwards out of the lane, hearing the scraping of branches along the sides of my car and praying I wouldn't hit a tree on the way out.

Chapter Fifteen

That night alone again in my room, my face fell into my hands and I pressed the heels of my palms to my eyes, pushing on them, willing them to pop out of the back of my head, so I'd have a decent excuse not to show up at school tomorrow. Facing Garreth's new attitude was too painful. But of course my eyeballs stayed put, so instead, I drew a deep, cleansing breath into my lungs and held it. But when it was time to exhale, I couldn't. It was stuck. Something had changed.

Then I felt it. A strange electrical impulse split the air behind me, worming its way up my spine.

Garreth?

It was familiar, yet not.

Different.

Alluring . . . dark . . . dangerous.

Then I knew.

I closed my eyes against the wish I had been stifling for so long.

Was it possible? A distinct flavor always seemed to float in the air when he was near, and it burned my tongue. It was deceptively sumptuous—the taste of darkness, of temptation; it immediately drew my eye to his tall, intimidating form.

I turned, acknowledging the presence in the corner of my bedroom faintly concealed in a shadow. I knew his dark eyes were waiting. I could feel them searing their way into me.

Reluctantly, I let my eyes roam, taking in more of the beautiful face that was silently assessing me, and knew that once I met his gaze, he would have me.

The moon broke through the thin vapor of the night and pierced its pearly light into my room. Hadrian stepped into its path, the glow washing over him with an almost magical light.

Clouds thickened and scattered, darkening and relighting his face, eerily playing with the scant four feet that distanced us from each other. I took a careful step forward, leery of the familiar shape that wasn't disappearing with the taunting light of the moon or shifting into a lie. Tonight Hadrian was not an illusion. His shoulders were set and rigid, but his eyes were . . . almost tender.

"How long have you been here?" I tried to control the shake in my voice.

"Days."

Days? I had felt it, the soft lingering of him creeping closer with each dream, each day that I spent away from Garreth. I couldn't help pulling Hadrian closer to the brink of my reality.

"I felt your mind." Hadrian interrupted my thoughts, answering the why that lingered on my lips.

"You felt . . . my mind?" I couldn't let Hadrian know how long my emotional wall had been crumbling; that I had become weak, defenseless, letting thoughts of him, the "what-ifs," seep out into the universe. That guiltily, I was waiting for this. I should have been more careful.

He appraised me for a moment, his eyes studying my face.

"I thought it was an illusion, the lucid dreaming that comes with being confined, shaming me into delirium. Hours turned into weeks, I truly believed I was going insane," he chuckled deeply. "Then again, I've always been a little off, haven't I?"

An invisible pole held me up just then because I was still having trouble digesting the fact that I was face to face with Hadrian. *Hadrian.* The dark angel the other guardians had feared. The very one who had planned the corruption of the angels and the destruction of the humans left behind. The one responsible for the disappearance of my father, and most likely Claire's accident. The one who had taken Garreth . . .

And yet . . .

I was truly convinced that somewhere buried deep inside him, his soul slumbered, waiting for the moment when the light would come through once again and awaken the guardian that only I seemed to believe he could be.

He stood still in front of me.

"Where were you?" I asked, trying to keep my voice steady.

"You don't want to know," he answered huskily.

"Try me."

"Hell."

The answer shook me. Images of fire and misery flashed before me. It's not somewhere I'd want anyone to go.

"How did you get out?"

"Does it matter?" He was agitated now and I couldn't help but take a couple steps back.

"I . . . I was just wondering." My pulse pounded heavily in my ears as I struggled to meet his eyes. I was the one who let go of his hand that night in the woods. The one who sent him into the darkness. Did I send him *there*? To hell?

Hadrian cocked his head to one side, as if listening to the rumblings inside my head. "It was Mathur," he said, as if meaning to put my guilt at ease.

"Mathur?"

It had never occurred to me to question Mathur's responsibilities. The high-ranking guardian in his flowing white robes had been a solace to me. He had enlightened me with the truth of my own judgment, existence, and purpose after I had followed Garreth to the realm of guardians, but my trail of thought was interrupted.

"Does this surprise you?" Hadrian asked.

"A little."

"Mathur was generous with my sentence, but I deserved worse."

I opened my mouth to protest, but his sharp eyes silenced me.

"You know firsthand what I am capable of; never forget that."

Then he softened his voice, "Images of you plagued me day and night. I realized, this was the price I was to pay for interfering with your life."

"*My* life? What about my friend Claire's life? *My father's?*"

"I admit to creating chaos, but I no longer find it amusing." Hadrian's eyes met mine cautiously as the fury I held deep inside threatened to burst. "I cannot control the havoc I create once it starts."

"Can't or won't?" I interrupted fiercely. I thought back to the night in the woods. The night of the fire when my hand let go of his and I remembered the look of remorse on his face as he plummeted away from me.

The space between us seemed to glow. The moonlight was fading, bringing the dawn closer, and I could see him more clearly now. His face was drawn, but still perfect. His eyes, dark at first, now reflected the golden tints floating through my window, allowing me to stare into a liquid emerald pool.

"You can't be here, Hadrian," I whispered. "I love Garreth."

"Really? Then why am I here now?"

If I looked at him again, I would weaken. Trying to stay centered and strong, I stared at my bare feet, now numb from standing in one place for too long.

He shifted one leg forward. He would be within inches if he wanted, towering over me, making me feel helpless. Stepping backwards, I tried to hide the wobble in my legs, which had grown unsteady under my still weight. He was quicker than me and I felt him gently grab hold of my shoulders, his eyes searching mine, reaching into a part of me only he knew existed. I couldn't break down, knowing if he looked deep enough he would find what I was trying to hide. Seconds away from losing it, I thought of Garreth, how he could manifest himself into the middle of this, but he was MIA.

"There are many layers to me, Teagan," Hadrian whispered. "I know a part of you believes or wishes that I could reform. But to deny all the darkness that remains inside me would be living a lie."

Hadrian took my scarred hand and traced his fingertip across the sweaty skin I had been clenching tightly. My mark greeted us in a swirling glimmer of light. It scrolled and extended, revealing itself in full splendor.

My mark meant "unity." I was the bridge between the realms, the societies. Angel and human. Heaven and earth.

Images of Garreth bombarded me, flooding my conscience. My first true love. But now, it was both painful and, dare I say, enlightening, that the truth was finally gripping my heart—that perhaps, I wanted Hadrian too? Part of me was like him in so many ways. The more I realized who he was beneath the dark façade, the clearer my inner self became.

I wanted to tell him I believed he wasn't as hollow and dark as he believed himself to be. I knew deep in my heart, no matter how guarded I had kept it from him, that despite everything he had done, he was probably more *human* than the average person. He understood the dark and the light each of us held inside ourselves. He understood that without one, the other couldn't possibly exist. We just needed the strength to see past the blackness and not give in to it. Hadrian was the blending of both and I wondered, could he possibly be the only guardian in existence to understand that?

Somehow, I always seemed to draw Hadrian back to me like a magnet. I found myself not wanting to choose between the two of them again. If I were to have two guardians—one light and one dark—was it to balance the light and the dark I have in myself?

I looked up at Hadrian, realizing he knew too.

He held my hand up higher.

"Have you not questioned the configuration of the mark you hold? Think, Teagan, what could it possibly represent?"

I stared at my mark, the one Hadrian seemed to know so much about. At a glance, my hand appeared scarred. Burned. But beneath the puckered, pink skin were three tiny open-ended circles, closely situated, in the formation of a triangle. Three scrolls coiled in the center of my palm, to be exact. They were connected by a thin line, much like a natural crease, embedded in my skin. I had often wondered why these markings had appeared in my hand. More importantly, why there were three. But I suppose I always knew. There was one for each of us. Me. Garreth. Hadrian. It was inevitable that the three of us should be linked.

"You once did the courtesy of saving me from myself. I need your help again." His voice, thick with emotion, charged the air.

I stared at him, not wanting to ask the inevitable.

"What have you done this time, Hadrian?" I whispered.

"Not me. Him."

My eyebrows knit together questioningly. I opened my mouth to ask, but Hadrian saved me the trouble.

"Lucifer." Hadrian's voice nearly broke on the last syllable, his eyes searching my face. "He's coming for us."

Chapter Sixteen

I shivered. My room faded slightly. "What did you say?"

"The one I have renounced as my brother seeks revenge, not only for the control I have tried to take from him, but for what I have become of late." My brain stumbled over his words, trying to process them. Was it possible that a greater darkness had indeed washed over Hopewell?

I had been contemplating a lot of things lately but nothing this frightening. Lucifer wanted to take over the corruption Hadrian had started . . . and then finish what I had started. Which was getting rid of Hadrian.

As unsettling as it was to have Hadrian stay with me while I worked his words through my head, it was also comforting my fear, and I was eventually able to get a little rest. When I woke, I was alone and realized that sometime during the night, a startling clarity had settled over me.

I needed two angels.

Simply allowing myself the guilty pleasure of *feeling* something for Hadrian was ripping me in half, literally. I swore Hadrian still had a soul, that he could be helped, and I didn't want anything to happen to him. But each and every time I felt myself being pulled closer to Hadrian, I felt the knife slicing me and Garreth apart. Even now, my feelings for Garreth were still so fresh. The fact that he was turning into something else couldn't erase my love for him. And I missed him desperately. To make matters worse, I still had Brynn to worry about. Somehow, I put myself in this position. Torn in all directions.

Maybe I deserved this?

I slogged my way through the first half of the school day. Taking notes, smiling here and there, appearing as normal as I possibly could.

During lunch, Ryan and I agreed to meet under a large spruce on the corner at seven-fifteen that night. Dinner would be long over. Brynn's wonderfully original topping bar would be praised for the umpteenth time and cleaned up by then. Probably by me. The evening would unwind, Brynn would grow restless, eager to meet her friends for the night and Ryan and I would perform our first act of breaking and entering. Really, what kind of person was I becoming?

Fate seemed on my side today when I encountered Emily in the same bathroom around noon. I had uncurled the wire from my spiral notebook in the bathroom stall and inflicted a nasty tear in my tights. Emily was mortified when I emerged sporting a run the size of the Andreas Fault line and a dead cell phone. She promptly encouraged me to borrow hers to call home for a replacement. While she was busy lint-rolling her own pristine pair of hosiery, I made a quick text to Brynn's phone about the party tonight. The one her friends were planning without her. I was hoping this would buy me and Ryan some time. Brynn would be vying to win back her position as head snob, while he and I rummaged through her house in search of the journal.

I crossed my fingers that it would work.

By the time the eighth period bell rang, I had decidedly set my brain into action mode. First and foremost, I had a ruthless beeyotch plotting to do me in and I needed to fight back. My angels would just have to wait, so I pushed my thoughts of them to the back burner and began to plan.

During my free period, I headed outside to clear my head and made myself comfortable on the bottom bleacher of our football stadium to mentally map out this evening's heist. I had been a guest in Dr. Dean's home only once and I was having trouble remembering the layout.

That's when my hand started going crazy.

The energy crackled high above my head, filling the air around me. I could feel the pull yanking me in two separate directions and turned my head to locate the chaos. Half of the football team out for practice was huddled near the far gate speaking to someone through the chainlink fence. That someone was Garreth. My Garreth. Even from the distance that separated us, I could see he had changed in the time that had lapsed since his authoritative hallway appearance. He seemed huskier. His hair was longer, which I suppose was normal, but he had a wildness about him that seemed to accompany his unkempt appearance.

Suddenly, it felt like the universe slowed, pausing for a moment. The guys continued their banter, seemingly unaware. But I felt something. And so did Garreth. His blue eyes found mine and only he and I were in motion. My spine tingled. There was recognition but no warmth.

After feeling guilty about projecting Hadrian back into my reality, I spent hours planning what to say should Garreth and I come face to face. Well, this wasn't exactly what I imagined, but it was close enough. All the questions, the thoughts I had prepared simply melted from my mind as I stared back at him.

And then the air stirred again.

I looked into the cool breeze. Beneath an elm at the opposite end of the school's property stood a tall, lean figure in black. I shook my head, mouthing the word "no," which fell silently from my lips as my books slipped soundlessly from my lap, my papers scattering beneath the bleachers.

By the time I exhaled the breath that had been lodged in my lungs, they had already crossed the field to each other. Derek Arnold was still and confused as he looked from Garreth, then back to the fence he had just been on the other side of. I made my way down onto the field, not sure if that was a smart idea but unable to stop my feet from moving closer to them.

Stunned, I tried to head off the confrontation. But what shocked me most was the look on Garreth's usually serene face. His jaw was set and his eyes, they were the worst. This newly found rage had transformed the iridescent aqua into a deep and smoldering storm.

Garreth turned to face me. I stood trembling, realizing his anger was now directed point-blank at me.

"What have you done?" His tone was ice.

I shook my head. *What could I say?*

I felt a presence behind me, then felt Hadrian's hand rest protectively upon my shoulder. I wanted to shake it off; to prove to Garreth I was still his. To prove I was sorry. But I couldn't find the strength to do it.

It instantly registered what I was witnessing. Garreth was jealous. He was fuming and Hadrian was reveling in it.

If only I hadn't believed that Hadrian still existed. If only my mind could have locked the door I never wanted to reopen . . . for Garreth's sake.

For my own.

But I believed there was something good about Hadrian. How could I ignore the truth?

Now I was the one paying for it.

"I see you've made a choice, Teagan," Garreth said, bitterly. I barely recognized my guardian when he spoke.

"But," I began stammering. My feet were firmly rooted to the ground beneath me, yet I felt like I was falling. His blue eyes, so tender a few days ago, glared back at me.

"What choice have I made, Garreth? Tell me. Because I wasn't the one who walked away." I was angry now. *Calm down, Teagan. Stand your ground; he'll come around.*

The look on his face was unrecognizable, but the pain in his eyes was deeply familiar. It was my pain, and it mirrored back to me now. It was obvious that Garreth was more changed now than either of us could have ever expected. There was no more room inside him to see the good in things, to see all sides, to give anyone else a respectable chance. Instead, it was all about him. His new emotions were raging through him like teenage hormones. Uncontrollable. Lethal. He saw only one thing now.

That I had made a choice.

And it wasn't him.

While I was busy trying to make right out of wrong, light out of dark, doing all I could to make sense of who I was . . . he was changing. This was way beyond what we anticipated. I thought he was pretending for me, trying to fit in. When all along right under my nose he was undergoing his own transformation.

"You've gone too far, Teagan." Garreth gave his head a sharp nod, pointing to Hadrian behind me.

Hadrian.

The culprit.

The instigator.

"Just couldn't let *him* go, could you?" He shook his head at me, then turned to look at his new friends; the rowdy football bunch, waving their arms and high-fiving each other. Only Derek stood a few feet apart from the others, confusion still evident in his eyes. But Derek wasn't the brightest light bulb in the box; he would soon stop questioning how Garreth managed to pass through a seemingly *impassable* aluminum fence.

I wanted to defend myself, but my voice was nowhere to be found.

Before I could process a response, I was staring at the back of Garreth's broad shoulders walking away from me.

What the hell just happened?

And then I remembered I wasn't alone in watching my guardian's exit. I turned around, expecting to see victory in Hadrian's dark eyes, but instead I was greeted with the most magnificent green, welled with sympathy and regret. Sometimes, Hadrian's eyes were black, obliterating the distinction between pupil and iris. Now they were emerald and clear with a scattering of intriguing gold flecks like an antique kaleidoscope. They were more stunning in the light of day than the green I had witnessed last night in the moonlit veil of my room.

I remembered seeing the first bit of his true eye color, when I felt him slipping away from my grasp. That night in the woods was one I would sooner forget, but for some reason, this moment seemed far worse.

The whooping and hollering grew fainter on the other side of the campus. Their voices blending together. I didn't even bother trying to find Garreth's; his voice was no longer his own. I instantly felt forgotten. With blind rudeness, I turned and began walking away from Hadrian. My walk turned into a sprint and Hadrian's confused voice was getting smaller by the second.

What did he expect me to do? I needed to be alone right now. I didn't belong here.

But this is my world, I thought to myself as angry tears formed. I looked at my hand.

Stupid mark.

I slowed to a stop, leaning over with my hands on my knees to catch my breath. Slowly, I tilted my head to look at the sky and shook my head, not sure where I belonged anymore.

Chapter Seventeen

Before leaving school, Ryan passed me in the hall giving me a "knowing" nod, and although the plan had been mine, I felt shaky and scared. Friday had come all too quickly, ending a week I swore was going to pass as slowly as molasses because of Garreth's absence. But Garreth had shown up in places I never could have foreseen and admittedly, my thoughts had been elsewhere.

I passed Brynn's hateful little posse, sans Brynn, and caught the tail end of yet another "Brynn bashing."

"She's so secretive now," Emily spoke candidly to Sage at their lockers, with little regard for eavesdroppers walking by. I rolled my eyes and headed out to the parking lot.

I drove home in a trance, hands gripping the wheel, eyes staring blankly ahead. I was on auto-pilot, but ended up home in one piece. What happened on the football field played over and over in my mind. The whole incident had left me with a residual numbness. I sided neither with Garreth nor with Hadrian. Subconsciously, I must have been siding with myself, sticking with my original plan of leaving my two angels on the back burner and focusing on what I had to do tonight, to save myself from Brynn. And to not get caught doing it.

101

It was obvious that Hadrian was going to be hanging around for a while and it was also obvious that Garreth had not changed for the better, both of which I had no control over. So, I resigned myself to the plan at hand of trying to appear normal while I ate with the enemy and then later still, when I would break into my mother's boyfriend's house to foil the enemy's plan.

My mother was still at work, although she would be leaving early to clean up and start the oh-so-original-pizza-topping-bar. After my stressful day, I decided to relax with a quick, warm bath before dinner. I filled the tub, still on auto-pilot, mesmerized by the swirling water at the base of the faucet, the steam billowing into humid clouds around my head. When the mirror fogged and the air was filmy, I turned the water off and let my robe slip to the floor. I stepped into the tub and lowered myself into the water, willing my muscles to unclench and relax. I closed my eyes and tried not to think of anything in particular. Just relax. Just me and the warm, soothing bathwater—at least for a little while.

But my brain tingled—something I didn't even know it could do. Before I realized what was happening, the steam cleared, letting me view a scene, a tangible vision of the one person I was trying to shield myself from. I saw Garreth as clear as day, hunched over in pain. Though my eyes raked over him I couldn't detect any sort of wound or injury. And then I felt his pain. Internally. Seizing. Gripping. My insides clenched and released in spasmodic jerks. There were no words for what I was experiencing, and just as the strongest swell of distress washed through me, he faded under the shadow of a dark-winged being so overwhelming it blackened every space in my mind. My terror redirected itself as an unseen force grabbed me by the throat and pulled me under. Just as quickly as it had come on, it disappeared and I was left face down in the tub, pushing myself up. Water spewed from my mouth as I choked for air.

I had died before, my subconscious reluctantly reliving the feeling, but this was different. This wasn't dying by your own hand to save the one you loved. This was dark, blackened hate reveling in the fact that you could feel your loved one's pain, leaving you helpless.

Shakily, I managed to step out of the now chilled bath-water. My plush robe did nothing to calm the tremors coursing through my limbs and I sat down on the rug at the side of the tub, pulling myself into a little ball, trying to calm myself.

Garreth, what is going on?

Standing up, I leaned my weight against the cool porcelain of the pedestal sink and stared at my reflection in the fogged mirror. Lucifer was returning for Hadrian. I saw the urgency in his eyes that night in my room. Was it possible Lucifer was coming back for more than just his brother?

Maybe Garreth doesn't know this time? Maybe he's totally oblivious to what's happening. Maybe his humanity is erasing the guardian in him.

By the time I felt sane enough to get ready and venture downstairs, my mother was walking through the back door. Four white pizza boxes balanced in her arms.

"Grab this would you, sweetie?" she thrust her left wrist out so I could take her purse.

She was overly cheerful, excited about the evening ahead, and for that alone I tried to hide the concern and fear still dwelling inside me.

"Let's get these pies into the oven. No one wants a cold dinner." My mother was a bustling tornado, opening cupboards, stacking seasonings. She barked hilarious orders like a crazed drill sergeant . . . "Open the red peppers!" . . . "Oh, my gosh, napkins!" For a brief moment, the pain and fear I had witnessed like a prophetic dream slowly slipped to the back of my mind, allowing me time to breathe and enjoy a rare moment with my mom.

Amid everything her cell phone vibrated and the preparations slowed. Her cheery voice confirmed that Nate was on the other end.

"He's on his way, but Brynn will be a few minutes late," she volunteered to me, then turned her attention back to the plates that needed to be stacked and the candles that needed to be lit. "Hmm, and I was hoping Brynn could set up the toppings the way she wanted, since it was her idea." Mom's hand hovered over the selection of olives and paused. "Well, she can rearrange when she gets here."

"Why is Brynn going to be late?" the sound of her name spoken out loud suddenly made the smell of pizza unappetizing.

My mom was still lost in thought, muttering to herself.

"Mom? Why isn't Brynn coming with Nate?" I said with a little more force.

Looking up, she replied, "Oh, she's just running a little behind. She took a bubble bath and lost track of the time."

My insides re-stiffened.

That was too coincidental.

Two hours later, my mother's laughter was the only thing getting me through the evening. Seeing her eyes bright and sparkling with happiness, so full of admiration for Nate, her newfound other half, I almost felt guilty for going behind his back. But then I felt the hairs on my neck stand in warning, and I turned to find Brynn dissecting me from a distance like I was a loathsome little bug in need of squashing. My guilt quickly diminished. It was a feeling I had endured all evening, from the moment she sauntered into the house, all through dinner and even now. My stomach was hurting. I didn't do well with tension, especially while eating weird pizza. It figured Brynn would play havoc with my digestive system, too, and I remembered there was one last can of ginger ale in the fridge. Maybe that would help.

Brynn's lip curled in disgust and I turned away, closed my eyes for the briefest of seconds and thought of Claire, who had been so different from someone like Brynn Hanson. The idea of Brynn somehow capable of entering my personal dreamscape, forcing me to see Claire plummet from the rooftop of a warehouse in the woods . . . I shivered.

My thoughts involuntarily returned to this afternoon, when lavender bubble bath permeated my senses instead of pepperoni, and my angel suffered at the hands of something dark and unknown. I took a swig of my soda too quickly, feeling the bubbles stream down my throat before I could swallow and the choking, drowning sensation took me off guard once again.

"Breathe much?" Brynn murmured from across the room, but I heard it loud and clear. As if she whispered the very words next to my ear.

She stood and languidly stretched her arms over her head, boredom rolling off her in waves. The highlight of her evening was probably making me uncomfortable in my own home, and I cringed at her success. Without a word she marched into the foyer and plucked her coat from the metal hook on the coat stand.

"Don't stay out too late, okay?" Dr. Dean called from the living room sofa, where he and my mother were enjoying a near empty bottle of Merlot, her giggles growing increasingly hysterical. It was time to escape.

"Not if I can help it," Brynn mumbled under her breath. "Goodnight Ms. McNeel! Thanks so much for the pizza!" And then with a sickening smile flashed for my benefit, Brynn opened the door and let herself out of my house.

I grabbed my own coat and followed her out onto the porch, my eyes darting in the direction I would soon be running off to, wondering if Ryan was already waiting for me or if he had chickened out at the last minute.

"Don't think you're coming with me. Our little "family" soiree ends here and now. Got it?" Brynn adjusted the brown fur collar on her suede coat and pulled matching gloves onto her hands.

"Oh, I wouldn't do that. I was just wondering what I was missing." *Please don't go home. Please don't go home.*

"I'm sure you would love to know."

Without another word she pivoted on her heels and sash-ayed down the steps to the curb, leaving me alone and shivering on the porch. Her car's engine hummed to life and I could see her gloved hand through the window, illuminated by the faint blue light of the dashboard as she fiddled with the buttons, knowing heat was warming her as my lips were turning blue. She gave a little wave, which I'm sure was accompanied by a smirk, although I couldn't quite see it, and then drove off.

I exhaled loudly, my breath pluming visibly before my face.

Opening the front door, I stuck my head in. "Going out, Mom. Be back later." I didn't wait for an answer to bubble up from the giggles in the living room, and then I too ran down the steps and headed in the opposite direction.

Chapter Eighteen

B rynn closed the door behind her. The lit candles
flickered wildly, casting eerie shapes across the room.
At last, she thought and a wicked little smile tugged at
the corners of her mouth.

Cradling the delicate cylinder in her hands, she breathed a
sigh of satisfaction and popped open the silver lid on one end
of the tube. The contents gently slid down the interior shaft
and into her open hand, waiting to be unrolled.

This has to mean something. It has to. Otherwise her stepfather wouldn't have gone to such lengths to hide it. Finding the
journal had been easy enough. After all, she made it a point to
know of all the nooks and crannies in this big house. Once she
opened it, however, she found herself confused and irritated.
Page after page mentioned Teagan's name, which only
bewildered and frustrated her. But she was curious about one
thing: reference to a sacred place secretly hidden deep within
the woods. It promised strong spiritual connection, perhaps
even magic, and described how people from long ago claimed
to have contact with the angels.

Magic. That was one promise that instantly caught Brynn's
eye. Everything else seemed boring. She carefully returned the

book to its hiding place and placed her attention on the map. Her eyes gleamed brightly with the thought of finding this sacred place.

Tingling with excitement, her finger traced the lines drawn on the map. Lines that led from what appeared to be a long winding road to a tiny church, because of the cross sketched above it. Clearly the map depicted trees. There were plenty of woods around here. She studied the paper, looking for any sort of landmark, but she was pretty sure she would be able to find it since the long road led to a river. There was a river just outside of town and a thick patch of woods about a mile or two inside the county line. That had to be it.

Gathering the rest of her "treasures" she had worked so hard to get, Brynn created her altar in a neat little pile in the center of the floor and drew a black circle around it with sand.

Black sand.

The delicious thought had come to her at the last minute, and she marveled at herself. How appropriate that her mother had vacationed on the black volcanic beaches of Hawaii with Nate. This was one of the few keepsakes she had left of her mother, of happier times.

All the more reason to use it, she thought to herself, forcing aside the tears stinging unexpectedly at the back of her throat. *Besides, a Sharpie or crayon would only leave a nasty stain. Oh, but the stain I'm leaving can't be seen with the eye,* and she giggled nervously to herself.

The candle's flame whipped violently, as if an unseen breeze had stolen itself upon it, and Brynn felt the skin on the back of her neck tighten and prickle. She turned around slowly, a trifle fearful, but the wicked smile returned to her lips.

She had never been one to favor a gamble. She was usually more ruthless than this, more direct, always in control of her calculated treachery and its ever-predictable outcome. To give up that power, even just this once was slightly nerve wracking for her, yet sweet in a sense. If this worked out the way she wanted, then she was more than willing to step aside. Especially relinquishing to one so *experienced* in such matters.

Brynn drew a gasping breath into her lungs and steadied herself. From the corner of her eye she could see the door slowly swing open, revealing the dimly lit hallway just beyond its frame. The door suddenly slammed shut, encasing the room in an icy stillness. There was no turning back now and there was no way in hell she was going to look scared and unsure.

Carefully, she set the map down inside the circle of sand and stepped aside, allowing the circle and offerings to take center stage, and then cocked her head to the side as if listening, knowing with a mesmerized gleam in her eye that the course of fate was about to change.

Chapter Nineteen

"Psst," Ryan whispered from behind a large spruce. "I could hear your sneakers slapping the sidewalk a mile away."

He emerged from his hiding spot and brushed the sleeves of his leather jacket.

"I got here as fast as I could." I leaned against a tree to catch my breath in the cold night air.

"Isn't your mom going to wonder why you didn't take your car?" he asked as we started down the alley that would take us to the cul-de-sac of Whitman Street and the impeccable home of Dr. Nathaniel Dean. I couldn't help sending up a silent prayer that Brynn had found her way to the party I tipped her off to instead of retreating back home.

"It'll be a wonder if she realizes I'm even gone."

Ryan shot me a quizzical look.

I lifted my hand and tilted an invisible bottle toward my open mouth.

All too quickly, Ryan got my point.

"Besides, she won't hear a car when I finally do go home and hopefully by then, Mr. Boyfriend will have left for the night and she'll be lost in sleepy land."

"Sleepy land?" Again, another quizzical look was shot my way.

"Whatever. Let's just do this."

There was no moon as Ryan and I walked silently, concealed in the dark. This was definitely something I would never do alone, even if I had a guardian angel watching over me. At least, when I had one watching over me. Even now, despite Ryan's company, I felt pretty alone.

I tried not to think of Hadrian's warning about Lucifer or my vision of Garreth in pain. Yet I couldn't help but wonder if either one was watching over me right now. Even if Garreth was still capable, would he be concerned for my safety?

I shook the unsettling thought from my head and tried to stay focused. I needed to find out if Brynn was up to something. Based on her history, my life might depend on it. And I needed to see the journal my mother told me about the other night. Ever since she let me in on Dr. Dean's secret hobby, I hadn't been able to get it out of my head. I needed to see what was written on those pages. Did he know about the secrets I was sworn to protect, the guardians, the markings? What if it was all there in black and white and the truth was beyond me now? Beyond the protective grasp of my tight little circle which included me, Garreth, Hadrian and Ryan.

Luckily, we lived in a small, tight-knit neighborhood, so the back door to Dr. Dean's house had been left unlocked. Slipping through the kitchen, we were as silent as mice. I had been here a few times with my mom but the rooms and halls certainly looked different in the dark.

"It's this way," I motioned, and headed down a dimly lit hallway. I looked back at Ryan, who was lagging behind, looking all around.

"Come on." I whispered loudly.

"This place is amazing. You sure this isn't a hotel?" He had stopped to pick up a bronze sculpture. "And why are you whispering if they're not home?"

His voice seemed to bounce off the walls, reminding me that we were up to no good.

"I don't know if they have housekeepers! Do you really think Dr. Dean dusts? Now put that down!"

Ryan reluctantly set the statue back in its place. "Yeah, I'm sure Brynn gets on her hands and knees to scrub. I'd pay good money to see that."

Rolling my eyes at him, I proceeded down the hallway to the door at the end of the hall, led by mere instinct that this was the way to the doctor's private study. I pushed open the oversized walnut door to find a lush wood-paneled office on the other side. The sheer opulence of the study took my breath away. Leather chairs, Tiffany lamps, ballister bookcases . . . the room was larger than my living room and looked like the inspiration for an Ethan Allen catalog.

"Geez," breathed Ryan. He did a complete 360, taking it all in. "If I could do my homework in here, I would definitely get all A's."

"Right, let's just start looking, okay?"

"Hey, Teagan. If your mom marries the doc, you'll be sitting pretty."

"Please don't go there. You know as well as I do this glam is not my style, and I would have to share it with you-know-who."

My fingers felt for the thin pewter chain beneath the shade of the desk lamp. With a tug, the light glowed steadily, revealing an intricate reversed painting on the inside of the glass shade. Beautiful winged angels floated in a gray-blue sky, hovering over a dark lake full of hands reaching for the heavens. Why would a medical doctor have a lamp like this? I shivered and began searching the desk while Ryan headed for the bookcases. I felt so nervous, my forehead was beginning to feel damp. The sooner we found the journal, the better.

"Someone's been here . . ." Ryan sniffed the air like a bloodhound.

I smelled it too, a soft lavender-vanilla scent was still faint within the room.

"Brynn?" Ryan asked.

"Maybe she stopped in here before coming to my house?"

That meant she was either still looking for the journal, or worse, she could have it on her right now. I headed for the filing cabinets behind the wet bar. Just walking past the crystal glasses made my head spin and I began to wonder if my mother was in over her head.

"No, I mean . . . something just doesn't feel right," he paused. "Don't you feel it?"

"Let's just look for the journal and get out. I think the whole we're-not-supposed-to-be-here thing is creeping you out."

But I could feel it too, something a little off, as if something other-worldly had tainted the very air we were breathing. I didn't want to admit to Ryan that the whole house felt strange, nothing like the last time I had been here. I shrugged it off, knowing the reason might simply be that the last time I had been invited. That certainly wasn't the case tonight.

I looked up at Ryan, meeting his unsure eyes.

"It's just guilt, okay?" I tried to smile reassuringly.

I pushed the hair out of my eyes and glanced at my watch.

"I don't see anything that looks like a journal," I sputtered disappointedly. I looked up at Ryan. He was looking around uneasily, rubbing his palms up and down his arms. Then I noticed my breath filling the air before my eyes. Ryan was shivering and I could see his breath too, as if we were standing outside in the chill. The temperature had plummeted a good ten degrees in a matter of seconds and a gray pallor had tinged the lamp-glow in the office.

The cold I was now feeling was nothing like before. It was nothing like when a guardian was corrupted and taken from its human charge. This was deeper. I was internally cold, as if something were creeping its way inside my skin. Invading me.

"Let's call it a night, alright? I can't stand being here any longer," I admitted and began walking toward the door. My sneaker crunched lightly beneath me, stopping me in my tracks. Kneeling down, I traced my finger over the glossy hardwood floor and rubbed it against my thumb. Black grit coarsely scraped my skin.

Ryan crossed the room to where I sat kneeling. "Guess the housekeeper missed a spot."

"It's sand."

At that very moment, the chill went deeper. Something felt horribly wrong. It was as if the walls had eyes and they were all focused on me and Ryan.

As we opened the door to the hallway, Ryan came to a screeching halt. "Someone's in the house," he whispered.

I stood staring down the long, narrow hallway, knowing it was our only way out, but my feet wouldn't budge. I was frozen with fear.

"In here!" Ryan tugged at my arm, pulling me into a coat closet, and quickly shut the door. "We'll wait it out in here, then we'll leave."

I could feel the darkness closing in around me like a living, breathing organism, filling the air with an unnatural pulsating thickness.

Ryan's boyish face was inches from my own and I looked at him now, wondering if he was going as crazy as I was. This tiny closet we had ourselves crammed into was playing tricks on my mind. But we couldn't move. Not yet.

"Do you think it's the housekeeper?" I asked quietly.

"I dunno. Why would she be cleaning this time of night?"

I had an awful feeling. "What if it's Brynn?"

Ryan just looked at me without answering. We both knew it wasn't Brynn. Something strange was happening in this house. Something . . . unnatural.

Ryan's face was illuminated by the flashlight I was holding in my unsteady hand and the light wobbled in various directions like a strobe light. The sensation of feeling seasick washed over me. A glimpse of jeans. My coat pocket. His knee. The wall. At last the light settled on his face. His skin looked pale and sickly in the yellow light. It reminded me of the night Claire took me to the rave.

Oh God, what an awful impression I had of Ryan then.

We listened to the silence, which is really a strange thought. If there's silence, then what exactly are you listening to? I suppose it was more a question of what we were listening *for*.

Ryan broke the hush, his voice gravelly, croaking like a wheeze. "Before my mom died, she told me heaven wasn't really a place. It's in our minds. We make our own happiness."

Garreth had told me the same thing. I wondered why Ryan's mom would tell him something like that. Maybe it was her escape from an abusive relationship?

"What if . . . what if hell was there too? What if it was all in our heads?"

We sat thinking.

Ryan rubbed his hands together. I imagined a tiny spark igniting between his palms. I imagined warmth and safety, but it seemed so far away right now. It was so cold here, but we had to stay. Just stay and wait. Wait for this terrifying feeling we were both experiencing to subside, or wait for Dr. Nathaniel Dean to return home to his strange, cold house. Neither one sounded like a good option.

I pictured a flame in Ryan's hands.

Hell.

Garreth once told me of a living hell, but that had been Hadrian's warped idea. Things were different now.

But still . . .

Lucifer's hell.

A personal hell created in each person's mind.

All it would take is just one tiny spark.

If heaven and hell were what each one of us envisioned, could the two co-exist? There would have to be a constant struggle between what was right and what was wrong. We all struggled with that every day; over what was good and what was . . . *evil.*

I looked at Ryan rocking back and forth on the balls of his feet, shivering.

He had a point.

And if that were true, then how could we ever escape it?

With bated breath we waited out minutes that seemed to stretch forever. Sitting crouched in a closet in still silence was pure torture. Finally, Ryan gave me a look that more or less signaled now or never and we made a quick and, hopefully quiet, break for the kitchen door.

Once we were out of the house, we ran without stopping to the corner of Claymont and Church. By the time we had reached the end of the cul-de-sac my lungs were burning.

"Holy crap," Ryan breathed heavily into the cold night. "I never thought we would get out of there."

My own heart was beating against the inside of my chest as I drew long breaths of air into my lungs. I was still cold, but not like before. Now I was shaky from feeling so afraid. It was a horrible after-effect. My house was a few yards down from where we stood and I was anxious to get home, to the quiet safety of my room.

I looked at Ryan. He was looking back at me.

"Should we try and guess what just happened back there?" he finally said out loud.

I shook my head. "No, I need some time to think about it."

And then in silence, he walked me home.

Chapter Twenty

The entire weekend passed by like a bad dream. I sequestered myself to my room, catching up on calculus homework and only coming out into the light of day to fill up on Skittles and frozen waffles. My excursion with Ryan on Friday had left me shaky and unsure about a million things and the best way to deal with it all was to be alone.

When Monday arrived, I was fully prepared to face the week as a strong, stable individual.

I should have stayed in my room.

"Sweetie," my mom said breathlessly as she tore through the kitchen before work. She looked frantic, flushed . . . so not my mom.

"I realize this is last minute, but Nate has taken a few personal days and wants to take me to his cabin up north. He's picking me up from the library. There's food here and I'll leave you money for take-out, but promise you and Brynn won't order out every night."

"You say that like she and I will be spending time together."

"Well, we're not going to leave you two alone. Besides, this is a perfect opportunity for you two to learn how to get along."

My mouth hung open, yet she continued to race around the kitchen as if the house were on fire. Then, just as quickly, she stopped.

"You'll be fine. It's only two days."

I responded with a blank stare.

"Teagan, please, I don't have time for this. I'm running late as it is already."

"Fine. Go," I murmured.

"That's my girl," and she patted my shoulder like a puppy.

"Just don't expect me to be alive when you come back." I had a sinking feeling in the pit of my stomach. A part of me wanted her to feel bad for leaving me here.

"Teagan, don't be ridiculous. Now, I have to go. Promise you'll keep an eye on things and that you'll try to get along? For me?"

Everything inside me shouted *No!* but I nodded, knowing it was what she wanted me to give her. She kissed my cheek, then grabbed her purse and a small suitcase and suddenly I was alone.

I thought about what she had just said, about not being ridiculous. "My life is ridiculous," I said out loud as I grabbed my backpack and locked the door behind me.

The plan was that I would follow Brynn home after school. Sitting in my car, I watched the other kids crossing the parking lot, making their way to their cars. Brynn was late, as usual, which was fine by me. I was in no hurry to see her, speak to her or step foot inside her house again.

Especially after Friday night.

I told Ryan about my mother's last minute plans at lunch, just so someone would know my whereabouts, should something foul happen. He stared at me sort of zombie-like, then said, "whoa, good luck." But today was definitely not lucky. Garreth had finally returned to school and the few times our paths crossed were wordless and uncomfortable. It seemed he was purposely avoiding me since the football field incident, choosing not to speak to me. At all. Maybe he was embarrassed? He certainly had lost his grip on his emotional control that afternoon. I saw him from a distance a few times during the course of the day, but that was the extent of it.

"Screw it," I said out loud and started the car. "Sorry Mom, but Brynn can fend for herself." For all I knew, she was sitting in her car a few rows back laughing her butt off.

Just as I was about to back up, I looked up and my breath caught in my throat. Garreth was standing in front of my car, staring at me. I turned the key, killing the engine, and slowly stepped out of the car. For some reason, I felt if I moved too quickly he would turn and leave.

He didn't appear angry, on the surface at least, but I couldn't tell. An entire week without him had made him feel like a stranger.

"Hey," I said apprehensively.

"Hi, Teagan," he said back and my heart leaped wildly at the sound of his voice. I missed him so much, but something told me not to let it show.

I walked toward the hood of the car, then stopped and leaned against it. I couldn't help remembering the other night in the bathtub, when I had seen a ghastly vision of Garreth in pain. He looked perfectly fine now—well not completely. His eyes didn't sparkle like they used to. He wasn't looking at me like he used to—but it was better that he wasn't in any physical sort of pain.

"Garreth, what happened?"

He looked away for a moment.

"I'm not talking about the drinking or the suspension. I'm talking about . . . you."

Warily, he met my eyes. "Everything happened."

"I don't understand." Was he blaming me for his own actions?

"I never expected to feel like *this*. I can't keep up with it all."

"Maybe it just takes time?"

"Watching the human race as an outsider is completely different from experiencing it firsthand. It's thrilling and everything I do makes me crave this unexplainable rush." Garreth had been toying with the zipper-pull on his black jacket, but now he was clenching his fists, grinding one hand into the other.

"Did you ever realize that it was also making you act like a jerk?"

As soon as I said that, he looked up, confused.

"I thought you wanted this for me?"

"I did. I didn't know it would *change* you so much."

Silence fell between us.

"So you brought Hadrian back?"

My eyes narrowed, feeling a defensive edginess creep over me. I already made my mind up that Garreth was just going to have to accept and deal with the fact that I had two angels.

"Seems that way," I said back, trying to sound indifferent.

"And you trust him? After everything he's done?" It was his turn to give me a hard look.

I looked him straight on and felt the tension between us rise again. I was riding on instinct here and was beginning to pick up vibes telling me to be on guard, but not about Hadrian. How could I admit an unexplainable trust was building between Hadrian and I? I centered myself and drew in a deep breath.

"I guess I do."

A shadow passed over his blue eyes and then something caught his attention across the lot.

I followed his gaze and saw Brynn slowly making her way over.

"Your hands are full," he muttered.

With a strong shrug, I squared my shoulders and replied, "I can handle her."

"I wasn't just talking about Brynn."

My mouth hung open as he ended the conversation by walking away toward his Jeep.

I looked over to see Brynn three feet away from me, leaning against a neighboring car and I quickly closed my mouth. Her one eyebrow and the left corner of her mouth were turned up, as if my very presence revolted her. There was something about the sight of her, combined with Garreth's new attitude, that made me straighten up and realize life wasn't going to magically readjust itself. That I needed to intervene and take charge.

"I just came to tell you that plans have changed. I have better things to do than hang out with you just because my dad asked me to."

Brynn's chocolate brown eyes tore away from mine and shot over to her friends. In the afternoon sun, Sage's caramel skin glistened exotically. She was chattering away with Lauren and Emily, who was impatiently looking over in Brynn's direction.

"Yes, I see your adoring fans are waiting for you. I wouldn't put much stock into how tight you are with them anymore. They seem to have loose lips lately."

"You have no right to talk about my friends, let alone think about them. Besides, my friends are nothing without me," she smiled smugly.

I could see them over Brynn's shoulder. Lauren was playing with her car keys, shifting her weight from one foot to the other. She mouthed something to Sage, who nodded in exaggerated agreement.

By the time Brynn glanced back they were gone. Three car doors shut a few parking spaces away and I caught a glimpse of three heads laughing inside the warm, leather interior of Lauren's Celica as they slowly began to drive away.

The look of utter shock seeped into Brynn's expression, but she quickly recovered.

"I'm meeting them later," she said indignantly, as if their taking off without her was a simple thing, and she began to fumble through her purse for her car keys. Giving up with a sigh, Brynn zippered her Juicy bag and gave me an unrecognizable look.

"Something wrong?"

As if admitting the truth behind her strained appearance was beneath her, she rolled her eyes and looked toward the school. "My keys are in Lauren's locker."

"Your keys?"

Brynn sighed with exasperation, "I stashed my stuff in her locker after lunch because it was closer to my AP French class, alright?"

I had to admit, seeing her squirm like this was highly entertaining, but it didn't erase the fact that Brynn no longer had a way home, at least not with someone she wanted to go with.

Visions of my mother and Nate in his sleek little Infiniti, driving along, talking about how his demon-daughter and I would bond over the next two days surfaced.

I didn't want to do it, but . . .

"I can give you a ride."

Brynn looked at me for a very long seven seconds, and sighed. "Whatever." With a hurried glance around us, she opened the passenger side door and slid inside. As soon as she closed the door, a thought came to me. Did Brynn feel any remorse or guilt for her part in Claire's death? Did it bother her to be in this car? Claire's car? I looked over at her but she just looked like she always did. Annoyed.

Chapter Twenty-One

The ten minute ride to Brynn's house was worse than getting my wisdom teeth removed in ninth grade. I thought the silence after my mother and I argued was excruciating.

I tried to break the ice shortly after leaving the school parking lot, only to ask if she didn't have her keys then how would she get into her house? I was dreading the possibility of having to spend the next few days with her, ordering Chinese and having to loan her my clothes. Fortunately, Brynn responded that she could get in through the back, and images of Ryan and me sneaking into her home on Friday night assaulted me.

I turned onto Whitman Street, heading towards the far end, where the road curved into the wide arc of a cul-de-sac. In the daylight, the gray dry-stacked home at 19 Whitman Street was breathtaking. A black iron fence ran the length of the front yard, breaking for the narrow flagstone walk, which led to an oversized arched doorway. It had black shutters that looked restored from an early nineteenth-century country home and a pristine yard full of butterfly bushes and wisteria that bloomed up until early fall.

Slowly, I steered my car up the long narrow drive that widened behind the house. Seeing the kitchen door made my palms sweat as I pictured the long hallway waiting behind it, the one that led to Dr. Dean's personal office and the tiny closet Ryan and I huddled in for what seemed like a chilly eternity. I expected Brynn to slam the door in my face and bound away, but instead she shocked me and offered the opposite.

"You can come in if you want," mumbling the invite over her shoulder as she headed for the door. I sat still, not quite sure I had heard her correctly. She stopped and turned towards me, the door swinging open to reveal the warmth of a French country kitchen inside. I suppose one doesn't take in too much detail when they're fleeing in terror.

"Well? Are you coming in or not?"

Part of me wondered if she had harmful intentions. Was a big kitchen knife waiting on the counter? Was this a trap to get me to admit I had broken in here Friday? My brain was one big sweaty mess, but still, I turned the key and the car's engine came to a peaceful rest.

I stepped into the kitchen, the pleasant scent of cinnamon greeted me. Brynn had already shed her jacket and was in the process of pulling her brown hair into a messy ponytail. I had never seen her with her hair up before. I had always assumed she was too snobby to look so casual.

Unsure of what to say, I stated the predictable. "Your house is beautiful."

"You've been here before."

Oh my god. She knows.

"The picnic in August? When my dad invited your mom and she made you come along?"

"Oh, yeah." I let the topic drop. It was a wonder she and I were even attempting to carry a conversation with each other.

"If you're wondering why the heck I asked you in, it's so you can tell your mother that we spent some time together, and you won't have to make something up."

Wow, I never thought Brynn would be into honesty.

She headed down the hall and I reluctantly followed. I'm sure it was my imagination, but as we ventured further into the heart of the house, the air felt colder. Brynn stopped for a second and looked at the closed study door with dark eyes, then proceeded to climb the thickly carpeted steps to the second floor, motioning that I should follow.

To the left of the Cinderella staircase we had just ascended, she flung a set of white double doors wide open, like a dignitary about to greet the press. Beyond was a stark room, polished and pristine in shades of white and little girl pink.

I gingerly eased myself down onto the white eyelet comforter of Brynn's king-sized bed. Brynn on the other hand showed no respect at all. She flopped down hard, pulled her knees up to her chest and sucked in a large breath.

"Nice room," I couldn't help feeling the uncontrollable urge to compliment. I never imagined I would be sitting on Brynn Hanson's bed after school. What would it look like to someone else? Like we were friends now?

I sighed.

Hardly.

It was too perfect to take in all at once, the lushness, the expense of it all. Obviously her room had been professionally decorated, unlike mine, and I made a mental note to myself *never to let Brynn see my room.* Unless of course, I wanted photos of my personal space plastered all over YouTube so the student body at Carver High could laugh. No thank you.

For as beautiful as her room was, it had a sterile quality to it, sort of a "borrowed" feel. I couldn't explain it. It just seemed the opposite of Brynn's personality. I really half-expected to walk in to find four black walls with skull posters, because that's what emanated from her on a daily basis. Not that she was a goth girl. Far from it. She was hateful and prissy and above everyone else.

I let my eyes roam over to the small white table next to her bed. A pretty seashell frame held the picture of a beautiful woman. She was strikingly familiar, and then for lack of a better conversation I asked the inevitable.

"Oh, is this your mother?" I wanted to reach for the frame, to touch it, as if my fingers yearned to hold it in my hands. There was something so warm and inviting about her smile. She projected an inner glow that was the entire opposite of Brynn, although they did resemble each other enough.

"Her name was Mary," Brynn's voice was flat.

In the photo, Mary was leaning against an iron railing, her timeless white pant suit accentuating her lithe frame. Birds hovered in the background, suspended in flight as if the camera's shutter had agitated the entire flock, making a stunning portrait.

"When was this taken?" I asked, looking for a conversation starter.

Brynn didn't raise her head. Instead she picked at a loose thread on her comforter, pulling and pulling without care, as if she meant to unravel the entire spread.

"She was on her honeymoon, in Italy."

"So your dad took the picture." I couldn't help staring at the beautiful woman that was the mother of such a piece of work.

"No, he was dead."

"I beg your pardon?" I was pulled out of the happy place the photo had transported me into.

"Nate took the picture."

"Nate?"

"Yes, I think you've met him. He's a doctor my mother married after the death of my father."

The facetious tone in her voice startled me, reminding me of where I was, and who I was with. Beneath the sleeves of my shirt my arms prickled and I felt the mark in my hand ripple, rising to the surface of my skin. For a moment, I had actually forgotten that we were enemies, that she was the girl responsible for many years of ridicule and grade-school torture. I could hear Ryan's voice echoing in my head that something strange was in this house, and here I was sitting on its bed.

Instantly, I felt self-conscious and very alone. My mother was out of town and no one knew where I was. Only Ryan knew of my mother's hope that Brynn and I would learn to get along, and I could only pray he would piece two and two together if I would end up missing.

"My mom died giving birth to Dr. Dread's stillborn spawn," Brynn hissed through clenched teeth. She switched her attention to a blue box she was now lifting out of the night-table drawer.

So that was it. The cat was out of the bag. Her resentment stirred the air, creating a thick soup of tension that pressed down on me. I understood now that Brynn felt abandoned, left behind to live with a busy stepfather who was devoted to his profession more than the girl he was supposed to take care of, leaving Brynn to be reminded of her loss each and every day.

I crossed my arms tightly in front of my chest, suddenly feeling tiny and cold and very out of place in Brynn's room.

"I'm sorry about your mom," I whispered, trying to sound gentle even though I was uncomfortable. I wanted to tell her I had lost a parent too, but I doubted she would care. This moment, like any other, was all about her.

Brynn shrugged, dismissing the fact that we were speaking of a matter that ran deeper than the surface.

"He tries to buy me—hoping I'll seem happier, but he has no idea." Brynn was whispering reflectively. This was a side to her I never dared dream of seeing. But here she was, strangely opening up to me. I was so used to disliking and fearing her, but in this tiny little window she had decided to open, I couldn't help feeling the ice melt a bit. I felt sorry for her. Her stepfather could buy her a Juicy bag, but it didn't mean it could make her like him. All it did was buy her way into an elite circle at school, the pent-up anger she carried helping forge her way to the top of the social ladder.

Brynn took a shiny bracelet from the little, blue velvet box and toyed with it a few seconds between her fingers. "Doesn't he know? He can give me this and that, but it'll never be what I really want."

The question formed itself on my lips, but I knew better than to ask. I knew what she wanted. I knew what her heart desired. She had steeled herself for so long, never letting anyone in to share her pain, her loss. But why me? Why now?

Her shoulders shook and she flung the bracelet violently into the corner of her immaculate bedroom. Poor Nathaniel Dean. He could fix broken bones and sew people back together, but there was one thing he would never have the power to repair. He could never fix the hole in Brynn's life where her mother used to be.

Brynn looked up at me. I had been sitting silent for too long, but what was I supposed to say? The poor girl needed someone to comfort her, to hug her, but attempting anything on that level would be crossing a line. I could see pain in her eyes, and for an instant I was reminded of Hadrian. Leave it to me to be blessed with an uncanny knack to see the depths of another person's soul.

Slowly, I rose to my feet and padded across the room to retrieve the bracelet for her. Brynn was distracted. She seemed to be lost in her own thoughts as she stared out the window. Perhaps she had revealed too much and wasn't sure what to say to me now? As I bent closer to the floor, the cool silver met my fingers, but that wasn't all my fingers found. Something black and coarse was embedded within the fibers of the white carpet. I pinched a bit between my fingers and felt myself recoil, rising quickly to my feet.

Sand.

My hand burned wildly in response.

Roughly, the drawer of the night table closed with a slam causing me to jump and spin around. The warm sorrow was gone from Brynn's eyes, replaced by something icy and almost ominous. My blood ran cold just then, and I knew I had overstayed my welcome.

Chapter Twenty-Two

My hand trembled as I pulled my cell phone from my purse. It was a good thing I had entered Ryan's number into my address book, because there was no way I could keep my fingers steady and drive at the same time. On a normal day, I would text, but today was anything but normal. It required hearing another person's voice, a live body on the other end.

Breathe, Teagan. Just breathe.

The instant he answered, I began rattling off the last hour and twenty-or-so minutes. I recounted seeing Garreth in the parking lot and the ever-growing distance between us, that Brynn got ditched by her friends, as well as the strange invite into her house.

"Are you okay?" he asked.

"I guess so." Really, I was fine, just shaky. "But Ryan, the sand. It was the same as what we found on the floor of the study."

"Maybe it's just a coincidence?" Ryan responded, but I could hear the worry in his voice. "I would invite myself over but . . . my dad is home today. Otherwise I would. You know that, right?"

"I know, thanks." I could hear movement on the other end, like someone shuffling. An angry voice boomed in the background that I surmised was Ryan's father.

"I gotta go. I'll call you later." Ryan breathed into the phone and moments later, there was silence.

I pulled into my driveway and walked quickly up the chipped concrete sidewalk to the back porch. The air was turning, feeling damp and chilly. I turned the key in the lock, eager to get inside.

Once I was in the calm silence of my bedroom, I threw myself onto the bed, closing my eyes to the day. I had been alone in the house a million times before, but today it seemed quieter than ever, and instead of feeling safe and secure, I felt tense and agitated. *It's just because Mom is further away than usual,* I thought to myself.

No, that wasn't it, although that was the case. Strange things were happening in Hopewell. Heck, strange things were happening to me. I took stock of it all. Brynn's befriending me for a day, the strange black sand in her room and the study, not to mention that Hadrian had resurfaced in my life. Then there was the tiny matter of Garreth, which deep inside my heart was not tiny at all.

It felt huge. Crater-sized.

I decided to head downstairs to boil some ramen noodles. After carrying the meager dinner up to my room, I settled myself at my computer desk and attempted to busy myself with schoolwork. But my brain wouldn't cooperate. Instead, I found myself opening my inbox and soon my fingers were typing a new message to Claire. At this point, I realized opening up to Claire was like a diary for me, soothing my anxiety, and the best part of all, was that no one would ever find my pathetic entries. My mother could come in and snoop all she wanted.

"Never underestimate the power of the delete button," I said out loud to myself.

After a quick email to my late BFF, I moved onto the book I was supposed to start reading for English. A term paper on Mary Shelley's *Frankenstein* had just been assigned and although eager for a good read, I found myself thinking about the real monsters in my life. I felt responsible for Garreth's behavior. I was the one who wanted him here, now, in this life with me. He knew being earthbound was venturing into the unknown and yet he did it, for me.

Garreth was changing. He was no longer protective, gentle, loving. He was jealous, reckless . . . as if he was now tainted by the very essence of human nature. What I found disturbing, however, was how quickly it came on. One minute he was fine, he was Garreth. The next . . .

I missed him terribly, but I still didn't know how to help him.

Just then the phone rang and I lunged for it across my bed, hoping it was Ryan.

"Oh, hi Mom."

"Hey, sweetie," my mother's cheerful voice rang out from the receiver. "I miss you already!"

"Me too, mom."

"Did you see Brynn today?"

"Uh, actually I did." I was biting what was left of my thumb nail. "We hung out at her house after school." *If that's what you want to call it.*

"See, I knew you two would get along." I stifled a snort under my breath. "Maybe this means Nate and I can sneak away more often?"

"Just not too often, okay?" I couldn't imagine another day like today.

"Are you still there, honey?"

"Yeah. Sorry, I'm just tired."

"Maybe you should go to bed early? At least stay in for the night. I heard a storm is supposed to hit. Well look, we're headed for a late dinner in a few minutes. I'll call you later, okay? Love you."

"Okay. Love you, too."

I pressed the little red button on my phone, ending the connection. My mother sounded happy.

I sighed. The thought of a chilly nighttime storm made me cuddle deeper beneath the covers. I picked up the borrowed copy of *Frankenstein* and settled in.

"Garreth!" I heard my voice call out to him, but he wasn't listening. Instead, he was doubled over with pain again. Only this time I was closer. I could reach for him—but he wasn't reaching back. Like he no longer recognized me, or he had chosen not to.

At last, his blue eyes focused on my face. He was speaking without words and I couldn't understand. I shook my head back and forth. Then the iris of his eyes turned black, obliterating the blue.

Suddenly, a cracking sound filled the space around us as Garreth attempted to straighten himself. I helplessly watched him struggle as pitch black wings began to extended behind him.

"Garreth!" I called out once again. He needed to turn around before it was too late!

Whatever was behind him was close. Too close. But as he stepped towards me I could see the wings follow him, and with alarming disbelief, I could see that he and the darkness were one.

I awoke with a start frantically wiping my damp hair from my face to see if the black wings were indeed real and were smothering me. A shimmer of light glinted within the scope of my peripheral vision. I turned my head. A shoulder and a wisp of blonde hair was all I could see before the image wavered and dissipated into the air.

"Garreth," I breathed into the dark. But it was another voice that answered me. I turned back to find Hadrian staring at me again.

I grabbed the blankets and pulled them in towards my chest.

"He's come twice today, seeking you," Hadrian's voice sliced the silence.

"How did you know? Are you following me?" I was sitting up now and perfectly awake, but I couldn't help staring after the now-faded image of my guardian.

"Yes."

I was about to ask why, but I didn't think it relevant to continue. Why *wouldn't* he follow me? I had practically begged for him to come back. Little did I know how my own thoughts would betray me.

My gaze wandered over to my computer, which was now going into snooze mode, re-setting the desktop background of a picture of me and Claire at the beach.

I looked up at him, "I write to Claire. It's stupid, but I email her. I guess . . . it comforts me. But you always show up soon after I send it. Why is that?"

Hadrian took a step forward. "Every thought is filtered to me now. It is a link you yourself created."

"*Every* thought?" I asked, cringing.

But he only looked at me intensely.

"Is Garreth in trouble?" I summoned the nerve to ask.

"Yes, your dreams are significant."

"But I don't know how to help him," I sighed, wrapping the covers tighter around me, partly because I was cold and partly because he was now standing right over me. I wondered if he knew about the feather hidden beneath my pillowcase? If he had seen my moment of weakness, of wanting—or perhaps he had been the one to prompt it. I kept my eyes averted. Although I wondered it, I didn't really want to know.

"You've saved him once already. Don't you think it's his turn to save himself?"

I stared at the beautiful angel in front of me, absorbing his question. Did Garreth need my help? If I didn't try, then who would?

"The human experience is overwhelming. Some cannot handle it when it crashes into them all at once."

"So really, this is my fault? This wouldn't be happening to him if he didn't become earthbound."

Hadrian leaned a bit closer, settling his green eyes on me. "I would do the same," he whispered. His hand reached out for me and caressed my face. "That, Teagan, is the unfortunate fate of us both."

As much as I felt myself drawn to his touch, I pulled away, conflicted. First, there was Garreth. Then there was Hadrian's cryptic message, *unfortunate fate*. What was that supposed to mean? I couldn't help feeling I had ruined the lives of two angels. Was I a disease or something? As my thoughts flew back to Garreth, Hadrian looked at me knowingly.

He straightened himself, regaining his regal stance. "You need to realize that Garreth is at risk. Anything earthbound is fair game now." His beautiful face followed the shadows Garreth had retreated into. "There are souls free for the taking."

"But what about me? *I'm* human."

"No, you're different. Lucifer fears you."

Puzzled, I looked at him.

"You don't know about the prophecy, do you?" Hadrian asked me and I shook my head.

He took my hand firmly and opened my palm. My mark burned and sizzled painfully before my eyes. The delicate scrolls of my mark blazed and extended toward each other, touching end to end and in an instant, my beautiful mark was changed. I stared down in wonder. A number eight met my disbelieving eyes. An eight, perfectly burned into the palm of my hand. Hadrian tilted it sideways.

"Lemniscate," he whispered wonderingly and his eyes met mine. "Surely you know the infinity symbol?"

I shook my head in confusion. "I don't understand. Why did it change?"

"Because the prophecy claims there is one who will come to bridge the darkness, allowing the wonder that is heaven and the simple ways of the earth to become one."

I looked at him, awestruck. Hadrian spoke as if he were reading from an ancient text, memorized eons ago.

"She will be the light," he continued, his voice resonating throughout my being, "and she is you."

"I don't feel like the light," I murmured. My thoughts were dark, full of temptation.

"That's because you are afraid to acknowledge the choices you are faced with. But in the end you will choose what's right, and it will save us all."

Chapter Twenty-Three

My mother's good night phone call had pulled me from Hadrian's gaze and when I hung up the phone, he was gone. I laid for hours contemplating the prophecy he had revealed to me. *If anything, I was destroying my own life with my choices and bad attitude lately.*

I drove to school the next morning, dodging downed branches and puddles the size of quarries from last night's storm. My quiet ride grew into a predictably mind-numbing day when I learned Ryan was absent. He hadn't seemed sick yesterday; in fact, he seemed absolutely fine. Grabbing the antibacterial lotion out of my bag, I gave my hands a quick cleaning just in case a virus was making its way around and made a mental note to call him on the way home.

He had seemed pretty distracted when we spoke yesterday. I had to admit, I was a little disappointed that he took the news of my after school trip to Brynn's house so lightly, but then again, I had been the one to offer her a ride home *and* had agreed to go inside. Maybe he was just being polite, not second-guessing my sense of judgment.

The funny thing was, whenever I spotted Brynn's friends, she wasn't hanging out with them. And when I did see Brynn, she was devoting her available time to someone else.

And that someone happened to be my guardian.

Lately, it seemed Garreth was hanging around her locker between classes, and I couldn't help feel pangs of jealousy and confusion when I noticed them eating lunch together in the courtyard. The very courtyard where I had first met Garreth. It infuriated me, but I didn't have any ground to stand on. I had brought Hadrian back.

To make matters worse, our parents were coming home tonight, which meant one thing: dinner. Not the usual come home from vacation, get yourself situated, read the mail, catch up on laundry thing. Nope. Dinner. The four of us. Blech.

With that thought I shut my locker a little more forcefully than usual and turned to follow the horde out to the parking lot. The halls of Carver High had been hideously transformed during the lunch periods, displaying poster after poster of the upcoming Fall Harvest dance this Friday. The gym was sure to be decorated with orange and red streamers and pumpkins and such. It seemed so festive that I considered asking Ryan. Not only did I find myself enjoying his company, it seemed any chance of my going with Garreth was out. Rumor had it, Brynn was going to go with him. The idea made me queasy. What the heck was he doing?

I groaned and unlocked my car door, slid inside and immediately dialed Ryan's number. The idea of doing something light for a change made me smile. It was a far cry from what we did last Friday together.

I pushed a Black-Eyed Peas CD into the rarely used stereo and waited for him to answer his phone, but it just rang and rang.

Odd, I thought to myself. *Maybe he's feeling better and went out?*

I pulled into the parking lot of Edward's to pick up a few things. Mom would definitely want flavored creamer for her coffee and I was craving Swedish Fish. I grabbed a green basket after entering through the automatic doors and headed for the back of the store. I found myself drawn to the Entenmann's pastry table, but an unexpected sense of worry hit me. Two older women were whispering next to the yogurt shelves, but I could still hear what they were saying, word for word.

"A shame, I tell you. That man should be locked up for what he did to that boy. It's just so hard to believe it was his own son."

"They were carrying on all night, Grace. I *had* to call the police. What was I to do?"

"You did the right thing. Well, at least Gunther Jameson won't be able to do any more harm from behind bars."

"Which hospital did you say that poor boy was sent to?"

"Mercy."

The basket nearly slipped from my grasp. My eyes followed the two women as they headed for the checkout and then my legs felt numb. I had to get out of there.

I made it through the self-checkout in three minutes and high-tailed it to my car.

Oh my god, Ryan's . . . in the hospital?

I could have kicked myself for thinking he didn't seem to care about my afternoon with Brynn. He told me his father was an alcoholic, but failed to mention the abusive part. I began feeling sick to my stomach. I raced home and sped to the kitchen, throwing the groceries inside the refrigerator. Then, as quick as lightning, I was back out the door. I still had a few hours before my mom was due home and headed downtown toward the hospital.

Finding a parking spot was practically impossible. For a small town, it seemed everyone was at the hospital today. I approached the information desk to find a woman in white scrubs, scanning a tabloid magazine over her black bifocals.

"Um, hi. Ryan Jameson's room, please?"

She studied me for what seemed longer than necessary, then checked the monitor.

"Room 312, honey."

I smiled a thank you and headed for the elevator. When I stepped out onto the third floor, a sterile smell stung my nostrils. My shoes squeaked on the floor. It was uncomfortable to be in somewhat familiar territory. The little plaque that read 312 was to the left of the open door and I could hear the steady beep of the blood pressure machine that was beyond. It reminded me of last spring, when I, too, had been a patient here.

"Hey," Ryan croaked, struggling uncomfortably to sit up.

"You don't have to get up," I said back, crossing the floor to the bed.

God, he looked awful. His face was puffy and swollen with fresh purple bruises along his jaw. It made me want to cry. His arm was bandaged but I didn't have the nerve to ask why. *How could a parent do this to their own child?*

"These are for you," I placed the yellow bag of Swedish Fish on the table next to the bed. My mother had always taught me never to show up empty handed.

"Well, now you know, huh? About my dad, I mean."

I nodded sympathetically, determined not to tell him he was the hot-off-the-press news floating around our local grocery store. "I'm really sorry, Ryan."

"Yeah, well."

I could now see the yellowing of old bruises lingering still on his arms and collarbone. How could I have never taken notice before?

"When will you be released?"

"Tomorrow, probably; my aunt's going to stay with me until the court decides what to do. This way school won't be interrupted."

I nodded. I knew Ryan lived alone with his father and that his mother had passed away a few years ago. Now I couldn't help wondering how she died. I sighed and looked out the large window next to his bed. It overlooked the parking garage and a small clinic. I couldn't help feel hopeful that Ryan's life would be changed for the better even while I was still stuck with mine.

"You okay?" he asked and I quickly pulled myself back into the moment, feeling guilty for pitying myself at a time like this.

I let my hand rest on top of his. "I thought that maybe, if you were feeling up to it on Friday, that you might want to go to the Fall Harvest dance? With me? Maybe it will take our minds off our problems for one night."

Surprisingly, Ryan's face lit up. "Sure, but I can't guarantee how good of a dancer I'll be."

Laughing, I smiled back at him, "I'm not a very good dancer, either."

"Then we'll make a good pair."

I stood up to leave. He was beginning to look tired and I had to get home.

"Hey, Tea." I spun around at his voice. "Are you sure you don't want to ask Garreth to the dance? You know, to fix things?"

I thought of Garreth and Brynn hanging out together today and bit my tongue.

"I'm sure."

Chapter Twenty-Four

"There you are! I've missed you so much!" My mother's arms wrapped me in a vise grip so tight, I had to strain to breathe.

"Mom, you've only been gone forty-eight hours," I uttered breathlessly, waiting for my lungs to fill again with air.

"I know, honey. I'm just not used to being away from you, that's all," and she squeezed me once again.

"So, where's Nate?" I asked, looking around the empty kitchen.

"He ran home. He wanted to check on a few pending issues in his office, but don't worry, he and Brynn will be over in a little while."

Don't worry? Why would I do that?

"He's picking up Japanese for everyone."

"I thought we were going out?" Actually, it was better this way. The thought of being seen in public with Brynn was enough to curl my toes.

I poured myself a glass of lemonade, while my mother sorted through yesterday's mail.

"Did you want to invite Garreth?"

I nearly choked. "Wh . . . what?"

"Garreth? Would you like to ask him to dinner? I haven't seen him in over a week, I'm starting to miss him."

At that point my composure must have given me away because my mother looked at me as if she knew the whole story. Which was impossible.

"Boy trouble?"

I could only nod.

"Want to talk about it?"

"No," I whispered, hoping she would let it rest. She nodded and picked her suitcase up and headed for the laundry room, leaving me alone with my thoughts.

It was seven o'clock by the time the second bottle of wine was opened. My mother was nestled in Nate's arms on the sofa, deciding which pictures to delete from the digital camera. Brynn was sitting lazily in the wing-backed chair, looking bored as hell. I swore time was purposefully torturing me, creeping along like this. I stood up and began searching for a means to occupy myself, like picking up the napkins that had drifted in from the kitchen, and fortune cookies, and crumbs . . .

I heard my mother get up behind me and then in a flash, I turned to see her lose her balance, nearly whacking her head on the bookcase nearest the sofa. Before I could barely blink, Brynn was up out of her seat, grabbing her by the arm and gently helping her back down to the sofa.

"Brynn, thank you. I guess I've had a little too much wine." My mother's face was pink and flushed. It was odd to see her so careless. No, make that *embarrassing*. I bit down on the inside of my cheek as the overwhelming urge to reprimand her swelled inside me. She was the adult, but she sure wasn't acting like it.

"You're just a little woozy," Brynn replied with a voice so gentle, I ended up doing a double-take. It was entirely out of character for her, and I half expected her to look up at me, smirking as she vied for brownie points. But her attention was one hundred percent aimed toward my mother, and in all honesty, it appeared genuine.

"Brynn's right, Diane. Just sit here for a moment." Nate began arranging throw pillows, placing the firmer ones on the bottom of the pile, the fluffiest near her head.

"I'll go get a cool, wet cloth for her forehead," Brynn chimed and headed for the powder room without even asking where we kept towels, or where the linen closet was. I was beginning to notice she was entirely too comfortable in the space I called my own.

In the midst of it all, I stood like a spaced-out idiot. I should have been the one to come immediately to my mom's aid. To speak softly to her with concern, to run for a cool towel for her head. But instead, I felt angry, even awkward in my own home, as if these people had come in and taken over things. Things that used to be mine.

"Mom, are you alright?" I asked, but my voice sounded strained, the question contrived.

What was wrong with me?

"I'm fine, honey. My head is spinning a little. Nate, I'm so sorry. I feel like a fool. I . . . I'm not feeling so well."

With that she pulled herself to her feet, pushing past the hand Nate offered her and staggered down the hallway to the bathroom. I met Nate's eyes. My own guilt and shame was overshadowing everything else I should be concerned with, like my mom's well being. She and I took care of one another. We always had. Always will. It was ridiculous that I should feel so humiliated when she was the one not feeling well, and I should be respectful and show my appreciation toward Brynn for helping my mom. Sure, Brynn wouldn't care if I was the one suddenly on the verge of losing my cookies, but she never had any concern for me. Yet, instead of rolling her eyes and using tonight's circumstances against me, she became the biggest help. Bigger than I was.

Brynn came back into the living room, washcloth in hand. The evening was over.

"Well," I projected into the stagnant revelry. "I'm sure my mom will end up calling it a night. She really should get some rest." *Finally! I was taking charge. Or so I thought.*

"Maybe we should stick around just a little while longer to make sure she's okay?" Nate suggested.

I bit the inside of my cheek. This was the first time the three of us had ever been in the same room without my mother. It was two against one, but remarkably, I felt okay. I felt strong. My mother was sick and I could handle this. I just had to feign politeness and get them to leave, then I could put my mom in her bed or on the sofa and escape to my room.

Sensing my discomfort, Nate walked over to me, placing his hand on my shoulder. "If you need anything, you can call my cell. It sends an automatic page to the hospital, in the event I get called in. You'll do that if she gets worse or if you need anything, won't you?"

I nodded, not promising anything. Brynn's moment of sincerity appeared to have worn off now that she was no longer needed. She stared at me—as if boring her way right through me. I couldn't tell if she was jealous or what. All I knew was that I wanted her out of my house. Now.

As Brynn left to go wait in the car, Nate grabbed his jacket from the coat tree in the foyer. It seemed like he was moving in slow motion. He seemed reluctant, hesitant.

"She'll be fine," my voice grew more convincing by the second. "And I promise to call if I need anything."

An approving smile of thanks crept into his eyes, but yet he still wasn't opening the door, and I imagined Brynn growing impatient, growling to herself in the car at his delay.

"Take care, Teagan," Nate said quietly. It should have been a normal thing to say. A polite statement of departure when you don't know someone too well. But to me, it seemed more than that, almost like a whisper of importance, carrying weight to his words. *Take care.* I heard it echo again in my head. What should I be taking care of? My mother? Myself? Was he warning me of something, because paranoid flashes of breaking into his study were permeating my mind, sending off warning signals. Did he know? Was I supposed to feel threatened? And with that, he stepped out onto the porch and into the night.

Chapter Twenty-Five

My mother spent the entire day in bed, calling off work for the first time in years. Before and after school, I waited on her, hand and foot, as restitution for my behavior the night before. I was sure she wasn't aware of the weight upon my conscience, for behaving and thinking so selfishly. I was silently punishing myself with each cup of tea I brought up to her, making her soup for lunch. Did she have enough pillows, an extra blanket? I threw a load of darks into the wash without being told. Nothing was enough.

I couldn't help wondering why and when my life and all its meaning had taken a turn for the worse. Was it when Garreth showed me that stupid pink suspension slip in his car? Was it the second I convinced him to go to lunch with a bunch of jock-losers instead of keeping him all to myself? Or was it the moment when happiness surrounded me and I had both Garreth and the free will to fantasize about a dark angel lingering on the fringes of my world? Regardless of when it happened, here I was…miserable.

"That's it!" I said out loud to myself as I tossed the last of the wet, lumpy jeans into the dryer. "I'm not going to agonize over this anymore."

I marched upstairs, peeked in on my mom, who was sleeping soundly in her room and fished my cell phone out of my bag. It was nearly eleven p.m. but I hit Ryan's number on speed dial anyway.

"Are we still on for tomorrow?" I breathed into the receiver without even asking how he was feeling.

"Uh, yeah. I'm up for it." He sounded as if he had been sleeping and suddenly I felt guilty for my impulsiveness. "You're driving, right?"

"The dance starts at six o'clock, so I'll pick you up at quarter to."

"My date's picking me up. I like it," Ryan spoke with unabashed drama.

I smiled into the phone and hung up.

Grabbing my jammies from the drawer, I quickly changed and hopped onto my bed. There was one more person I wanted to call, but unfortunately, he didn't carry a phone. At least to my knowledge. I thought of what Ryan said, about thinking about Claire and then seeing her. If I thought about Garreth, would he come to me? Did I dare try? I wasn't going to allow myself to feel bad if he chose not to appear. The important thing was that I was reaching out and trying to put my life back into some sense of order.

I visualized him forming in the middle of my bedroom floor like he had done so many times in the early morning. I closed my eyes and wished.

Nothing.

But someone else did enter my dreamscape this time. Claire stood there with a worn, brown book in her pale hand. It was old and frail, and in my heart I knew it was the journal I was looking for.

"I kept him away for as long as I could, Teagan. I don't have the strength anymore," the wisp of her voice floated to me.

"Who, Claire? Who did you keep away?" I asked, but she was fading before my sleepy eyes.

"The names . . . the names are in the book." I could no longer see her, but her voice punctured my heart.

"What names?" I pleaded, but she was gone.

When morning woke me, I didn't feel so alone. I had seen Claire. Feeling the separation from her had weighed on me with such magnitude, but seeing her, even just for a matter of moments in a dream, helped. I truly believed that she was giving me a message—that the journal really held importance. I carried that thought with me while getting dressed and on the way to school.

There was a tangible excitement in the air at Carver. It was Friday. The Fall Harvest dance was just a few hours away and the school was already teeming with festivities. Girls chattered in the bathroom, talking about their dresses and shoes and hair. Even the boys seemed stoked. By the time the final bell rang, even I was admittedly feeling the effects of anticipation and found myself practically bouncing to my car. Both Garreth and Brynn were no-shows today. I didn't have to witness their *togetherness,* which helped. Out of sight, out of mind, right?

At five forty-five my little white Cabrio pulled up to the house Ryan had described over the phone. I had never been there before but ventured to guess that it wasn't the sort of place where someone would entertain. The pale blue siding had faded to a nice shade of dinge. The white trim was now visibly grimy, even from the street, and in need of a good power-washing. It was peeling profusely around the door frame and windows.

I sat in the car, not entirely eager to get out and approach the front door. Even though his father wasn't home, I felt more inclined to sit and wait patiently while I played with the trim of my dress. I had been reluctant to wear the blood orange party dress. It was the one I had worn to my birthday dinner with Garreth but also the only thing appropriate in my closet for this evening. Perspiration beaded up on my palms at the thought of running into him tonight, especially with Brynn by his side.

I shoved the idea from my thoughts. No sense in ruining the night before it ever got started. I debated running up to the door. Ryan sure was taking his time tonight. Wasn't it more customary for the boy to go up to the door? Did the same rules apply when the girl was the one driving? I half-smiled to myself as I pictured getting out and holding the door open for him.

A few minutes later, my wait was over and Ryan appeared on the tiny porch wearing a nice pair of pants, a blue dress shirt and . . . was that a tie? A petite woman with a blonde bob stood in the open doorway and I rolled my window down to give a little wave to whom I assumed was his aunt and current guardian.

Getting in, Ryan seemed to be blushing.

"Nice tie," I muttered.

"My aunt talked me into it," he said hesitantly.

"Seriously, it's a nice look for you," I said, nodding emphatically, not wanting him to think I was teasing. I meant it. "Are you sure you're feeling up to tonight? We could go for coffee instead if you'd like." I could still see some bruising around his jaw, but in the dark gym no one would notice. I realized then that was probably the real reason for the tie, but I didn't let on.

"Oh, I almost forgot. This is for you." Shyly, Ryan handed me a beautiful corsage of pink roses and baby's breath. "It's supposed to go on your wrist."

The gesture caught me off guard and made me smile.

"Thank you. Ryan, that was very sweet of you!"

"I guess my aunt was hoping you would come to the door. She wanted to get a couple of shots with her camera."

"I'm sorry, I ..." I stammered guiltily.

"It's okay, she'll get over it. I told her it was just a dance, not the prom."

This time it was my turn to blush. I held my arm out across to him and shivered slightly as he pulled the elastic cord around my hand and up onto my arm, adjusting it on my wrist.

"It's just perfect, Ryan. Really."

I updated him on my last conversation with Hadrian as we drove. Ryan's reaction to the whole guardian scenario was quiet and supportive. He listened without interrupting, making me realize how much I truly appreciated the friendship we had developed.

Music caressed the night as it wafted out from the double green doors of the gymnasium. From a distance streamers and silver strings of lights could be seen, creating a stunning wonderland, a far cry from the sweat-infused room we visited twice a week. Ryan and I stood quietly in line trying to avoid the stares. Was it really so strange that I would show up without Garreth? Was it even stranger that Ryan would accompany the friend of a former girlfriend? Probably. We paid the ten dollar donation at the door that bought us two raffle tickets for door prizes and quickly shuffled inside.

A few daring couples were already on the dance floor, twirling in front of those watching from the sidelines. There were long tables draped in autumnal swaths of fabric with punch bowls and bottles of water. Other tables held cakes and brownies and other delectable treats provided by over-achieving mothers and PTA members. The music was loud, coming from a corner that had been transformed into a mock sound stage and several DJ wanna-be's were hovering close by offering the next suggestions to spin.

I let out a sigh.

"You okay?" Ryan looked at me with genuine concern.

I nodded. "I just feel a little out of place, that's all."

"Would you rather leave? I don't mind," he said, pulling at the knot at his collar.

"No, let's stay for a little bit. I'm sure it will be fun," I tried to sound convincing. "It really looks amazing in here, don't you think?"

"Yeah, but it still smells like socks."

I punched him lightly in his good arm.

As much as I tried, my eyes couldn't help searching the far reaches of the gym for Garreth. I cursed myself for being so masochistic.

I excused myself to the ladies' room and once inside the safety of a stall, I took deep, calming breaths. I hung my head in my hands, trying to stop thinking about my blond-haired guardian who should have been with me tonight.

Looking at my hand, I traced the lemniscate with my finger. It was mesmerizing to keep curling around, over and over. I still couldn't fully understand why my mark had changed, or what it meant. A deep part of me was angry that Garreth hadn't been with me when it reshaped itself, like he had been the first time. I held some sort of feelings for Hadrian—there was no way around denying that—but the hole where Garreth used to be seemed to be getting larger.

Stepping up to the sink, I splashed some cold water on the back of my neck and took another deep breath. Tonight, I would try to forget about Garreth and the strange dreams about dead friends and old books. I was determined to have a good time and not let Ryan regret being my date for the evening. My hand reached out in front of me pushing hard on the heavy bathroom door.

Stupid door. . . what is your problem? And then with one final push, it swung open with a thud. When I looked up, I was standing face to face with Brynn, holding an empty punch cup, the red contents now staining the front of her cream colored designer dress.

"You IDIOT," Brynn stammered lividly. Several eyes were upon us now and I couldn't tell if the stream of cool wetness running down the back of my neck was from the water I had just splashed on myself or sweat from embarrassment.

"Oh, Brynn! I'm so sorry. Your dress. I'm sorry!"

She held it out in front of her, making the hideous stain larger than it really was. It looked as if blood had been spilled all down the front of her and reminded me of that scene from the movie *Carrie*. The one where pranksters spilled pig's blood over Carrie's head. Except no one was laughing at the girl with the red stain right now. No one would *dare* laugh at Brynn Hanson.

The last thing I saw were dozens of nameless faces rubber-necking for a good view of the ensuing argument before the bathroom door closed once again. I felt a hand grasp the bodice of my dress and push me backwards, slamming me against the dryer that jutted out from the tiled wall. My breath was knocked out of my chest.

"I said I was sorry about the dress," I repeated through clenched teeth.

"You should be sorry about a lot of things," Brynn spat.

I couldn't even begin to wrap my head around that one, it was hurting too much.

"I'll pay for the dress . . . have it dry cleaned or something. Where did you get it, Dehlia's?"

Brynn didn't answer but instead stood staring at me for a moment, then reached out and grabbed a handful of my hair.

"Hey!" I shouted. "Back off!"

But she kept pulling and twisting harder.

"Stop it! You're hurting me." I managed to squeak out, but her grip held firm. She looked possessed. The Brynn she revealed to me in her bedroom was long gone. Why wasn't anyone coming in to pull her off of me? Where was Ryan? Wasn't he wondering what was taking me so long? If I made it out of here, I'd be lucky to still have a strand of hair left on my head!

From out of nowhere, a brilliant white glow streamed from my hand, accompanied by a surge of strength that moments before had not existed.

"I said stop!" And with that, I finally pulled myself free and pushed her away.

An eerie silence filled the room and flowed beyond the closed door. Suddenly, it flew open and Ms. Hodges, the assistant principal stood in the doorway with a stricken look plastered across her face. Flanking her on either side stood Ryan and Garreth, their eyes wide and worried.

"I expect an explanation. NOW." Ms. Hodges was obviously not in the mood.

I completely expected Brynn to place the entire blame on me. I did, after all, open the door on her.

"Teagan was . . ."

I held my breath waiting for the verbal blow Brynn was about to deliver.

"Teagan was only helping me clean off my dress. It looks much worse than it really is." With that, she dabbed her dress with a damp paper towel.

My jaw hung open to the floor but shut quickly when Ms. Hodges looked at me for my side of the story. I simply nodded in agreement.

We marched out in single file, avoiding the stares of everyone at the dance.

"I trust there will be no more antics this evening?"

Brynn and I bobbed our heads in unison.

"Alright everyone! There's nothing to see here, a minor glitch in the festivities this evening." She clapped her hands and gave a nod toward the sound stage and soon the room was filled with music and laughter and whispered voices.

I turned to Brynn. "I really am sorry about the dress." I didn't want another argument—we'd get kicked out for sure—but I had to ask. "Did you have to grab me like that?"

Brynn looked at me with large brown eyes. "I didn't grab you," she said innocently.

My brows furrowed together and I reached up to touch the mess on top of my head. Ryan was at my side in a nano-second, shaking his head, staring at us both. "You guys were in there for two seconds and you come out like this."

It was longer than two seconds. I was sure of it, and if Brynn was pretending to not remember anything that happened, she was doing an awfully good job.

My eyes met Garreth's and I could feel myself getting trembly again. He looked amazing and serene. Maybe he was getting better? I wanted to step toward him but Brynn came to his side, reminding me that he was her date tonight. Not mine. Did he even still care? A gentle arm wrapped around my shoulder, and I knew Ryan was trying to be protective.

"Coffee sure sounds good, doesn't it?"

I looked up into Ryan's dimpled grin. "It sure does."

One last glance at the gym and I could see Brynn pulling Garreth onto the dance floor, her ruined dress momentarily forgotten. I gave Ryan's hand an appreciative squeeze as we walked out the door of the gym and into the dark night dotted with millions of tiny stars.

Chapter Twenty-Six

The mug was warm in my hands. It felt too good to put down. I took another sip and sighed.

Ryan was staring at me. "Okay, tell."

"Tell what?"

"The bathroom. Brynn. Go on with it."

I sighed again and took a look around. Most of the tables were empty and only a few customers were up at the counter.

"The door was jammed so I pushed. I had no idea she was on the other side, and it made her drink spill down the front of her dress. Then, she freaked."

"Define freak." He was leaning forward on his arms now, giving me his full, eager attention.

Beneath the table I traced the inside of my palm with my finger.

I scrunched my face, trying to recall exactly. "She wigged out. She pulled my hair and pushed me against the wall. Actually, it was in the opposite order. She was really strong. And her face was . . ."

I couldn't finish and he didn't press me. He just looked at me across the table ignoring his black coffee. I wondered silently if this had anything to do with the so-called prophecy.

165

Was this really hell as Ryan had questioned in the closet, and as Hadrian seemed to confirm the other night? Part of me simply wanted to believe that Brynn was a stark-raving lunatic who needed to be institutionalized immediately. Her father was a doctor; couldn't he see the signs?

"She doesn't hang out with her friends anymore," Ryan volunteered.

"I know. They seem to have ditched her."

Ryan finally took a sip of his coffee. "She's keeping company with Garreth lately, huh?"

Instead of answering, I looked down and played with my napkin.

Do I tell him? About the prophecy? Would it scare him if I said that every thought he spoke out loud about hell was indeed real?

My head was killing me.

Ryan leaned over and whispered very softly, even though there was no one around to hear.

"I had a dream about Claire again last night."

I looked up.

"She said you were the answer."

"The answer to what?" I whispered back as the hairs on my arms began to stand.

"I have no idea." Then he reached over, took my hand and carefully opened it. Hadrian had called it a lemniscate. I sighed. There it was—an eight lying sideways across my palm.

Infinity.

I sucked in my breath, waiting for the slew of questions to stream from across the table. I had never let Ryan inspect my mark so closely before, always playing it up that it was simply a burn, and that to touch it gave me the willies.

"You hold forever in your hand," Ryan said quietly. The funny thing was, he didn't seem too surprised. I wondered if his dream about Claire had prepared him in some way?

The outside pocket of my purse vibrated, and I reached down to retrieve my phone.

My mother's voice was practically frantic on the other end. "Teagan, are you alright?"

"I'm fine, Mom."

"Nate called me." *No surprise there.* "He said Brynn's missing."

"Relax, Mom. She's probably still at the dance." I didn't bother mentioning who she was whirling and twirling across the dance floor with.

"Honey, the dance ended forty-five minutes ago. Where are you?"

I yanked Ryan's arm toward me and fumbled for his watch beneath his sleeve. How long had we been sitting here? "Sorry, we stopped for coffee. I didn't realize what time it was."

"Please, Teagan, will you just run over to his house and help him? He said he would meet you there in fifteen minutes. I'd go myself but I'm still not feeling all that great." She did sound tired, which made me wonder if it was more than an extended hangover. Maybe she had the flu?

"Brynn's a big girl. I'm sure she'll show up eventually." I was getting exasperated. What was I now? Her keeper?

My mother grew silent on the other end.

"Mom?"

"Please, just do this for me. I'm worried about Nate."

"I thought you were worried about Brynn?"

Again, there was silence and then my mother's voice could be heard softly in my ear. "It's the anniversary of her mother's death, honey. Every year she takes it harder and harder."

What could I say to that, besides agree to go? Even though it was the last thing I wanted to do, even though the thought of setting foot inside that big, creepy house at night made me shiver.

Ryan gave me a raised eyebrow, which translated meant "fill me in, I'm clueless."

I hastily explained, grabbing my keys.

"Think she's with Garreth?"

I shrugged. Who knew? If they were missing, maybe they didn't want to be found, and right now, I didn't want to be the one to stumble upon them and shout *oh there you are!*

Much to his dismay, I insisted on dropping Ryan off at his house. I could see he was wearing thin. The evening had done him in and I couldn't bring myself to be responsible for slowing down his recovery. Besides, perhaps it was time to put this prophecy business to the test. When I pulled up to the stately home of Dr. Dean, I took note that only two lights were on. One was the front porch light, perhaps left on for me, and the other was gleaming dimly through the heavy designer draperies on the east side of the house. I ventured to guess that the good doctor was busying himself in his study while he waited for me and the return of his stepdaughter.

Great, my favorite room of the house.

The entire ride over, I repeated the same phrase in my head. *I'm doing this for my mom. I'm doing this for my mom.* Now that I had arrived, it was safe to say that the little pep talk did nothing to squelch my butterflies. Either that, or the strong coffee I had nursed for nearly an hour was beginning to kick in.

My footsteps echoed on the flagstone walk as I treaded up to the doorbell, my orange dress billowing in the breeze. After a few tense moments, the door swung open and there stood Nate looking troubled, flashing a forced smile.

"Glad you could come. Your mom called to say you were on your way."

I stepped inside, once again taking in the sparkling opulence of his home.

"I have a feeling I know where to find her," he uttered, closing the heavy front door.

"Um, if you don't mind my asking . . . if you know where she is, then why do you need my help?"

Without answering, he motioned for me to follow him down the hall, straight towards the one room I had no desire of ever stepping foot in again. A feeling of déjà vu swept over me. Once more I was reluctantly following someone in this house, and I wasn't too happy about it.

The study was in a state of disarray. I sucked my breath in and looked around, confused by the papers and books strewn about. Volumes of collectible journals and manuscripts bearing medical insignias were scattered. The desk, immaculately organized the last I had seen it, was now covered with papers and various files.

Dr. Dean was disheveled as well. His shirttails were half tucked in, half pulled out of his trousers. His clothing was wrinkled and appeared slept in, matching the stubble growing on his face. He ran his hand wearily through his tousled hair, messing it up even further.

"Are you alright?" I asked.

"It's been a long night." His voice usually had a soft spoken tone but tonight it was rough and gravelly. Maybe he was catching whatever my mom seemed to have. He stood staring at the mess around us, shaking his head.

"Who did this?"

Dr. Dean tore his gaze from the chaos to meet my eyes. "Actually, I did."

There must have been a strange look on my face because he immediately answered, "I was looking for something. A map I believe Brynn took with her tonight before disappearing."

With a deep and weary sigh, he continued. "There's a journal I keep. It's very important to me. Beyond representing my devotion as a doctor, this journal is my life's work, and it seems Brynn has made every effort to try and find it."

Did Brynn have the journal? My thoughts raced as I pictured her reading the secrets contained within its pages.

"No need to be worried, Teagan. I've hidden the book well and am sure it's quite safe. The map is an exact replica of one in my journal and is, unfortunately, no longer here."

"Was it . . . someplace special? The place the map leads to?" I felt uncomfortable asking, especially knowing the map had ties to the journal, but I quickly reminded myself that he was the one who asked for my help finding Brynn. It would seem running off to the cemetery or perhaps visiting a place that held special meaning to her, or reminded her of her mom, would have made more sense than following an old map.

Dr. Dean sat down at his desk and fiddled with the marble paperweight, picking it up and setting it down on the jumble of papers there, over and over again.

"There have been stories of sacred places handed down through the years, many of which I have recorded in my journal. I happen to be very fond of ancient spiritual lore. This map supposedly leads to such a place, one of great mystery and power. With her mother gone for a few years now, there's no doubt Brynn is searching for something fulfilling."

The paperweight landed squarely with a final thud.

"I'm sorry, but where exactly do you think we should start looking for her?" A nagging impatience hit me suddenly, making me anxious to head out, but still, his words echoed in my head. *Sacred place. Ancient lore. All recorded in his journal. He knows*, my subconscious warned. *He knows about guardians.*

All too quickly, the room felt excruciatingly warm. The fireplace had felt nice when I first came in from the chilly night but now seemed to exaggerate the uncomfortable alarm stirring inside me. My thumb found the inside of my hand, feeling the impression inlaid there as an old familiar tingling began to surface on my skin. Was it warning?

Dr. Dean's eyes, bright from the fire's glow reflected in them, zeroed in on mine. It was as though he had something extremely vital to say to me. Something for my ears alone and I had no idea what to expect. I clenched my hand tightly. Had he seen me rubbing the mark on my hand? It was an instinctive thing of late that I reached for the marking etched there, as if my touch could calm the building tremor within my skin and soothe the sense of warning that often came on so strongly.

But instead, he crossed the room to the bookcases where a rather obscure shadow box hung on the wall. Dr. Dean turned to me and quietly motioned that I too should be inspecting this little shelf-like box. I had never noticed it before, so easily it blended in with the deep tones of the wooded bookcases. It seemed to be filled with knick-knacks, little things that were perhaps precious and meaningful but that went unnoticed stored in the depths of the interior compartment. In the sparse lighting I could make out a small stack of postcards from Hawaii, a small box adorned with shells and beads and several lumpy rocks I assumed were lava.

"She hates me," Dr. Dean said quietly. "She believes I took the most important thing from her, which I suppose I did."

I looked up at him, standing still by my side. In the dim of the room he appeared wearier than ever.

"Brynn wants nothing to do with me or with what I consider to be important. So, of course, I always assumed this was the best place to hide what means the most to me." I watched as he reached up allowing his hand to disappear into the depths of the box, pulling from it a smooth brown, leather book. It was the journal and by his words, had possibly been safe from Brynn's prying eyes all along.

I internally questioned why Brynn would want the book in the first place, but remembering the sand on the floor and in her room, I swallowed my urge to ask.

It seemed that the moment the journal was removed from its safe hiding place, the flames in the fireplace swelled higher—as if boasting or challenging the book itself. My head was playing tricks with me again and I tried to focus on the smooth leather book Nate now held in his hands.

He took a step closer to me. The flicker from the roaring fire was making the room spin. I was having trouble thinking.

"You're not alone in all this."

I looked up at him and a familiar kindness sparkled in his gray eyes, but I couldn't bring myself to rely on it. Not yet.

Without a word, he held his right hand out to me and a shudder seized my body. I stared at his hand in disbelief. He stood patiently, giving me time to process what he was revealing, and then tentatively took my hand and brought it up next to his own. They were nearly identical. He shook his head and smiled, acknowledging what I couldn't speak.

"There are others like us."

The symbol of unity etched into his hand was faded and worn, maybe because he was a grown man and I still had the smooth hands of youth. I shook my head . . . so many questions.

"It developed when I was eleven years old. I never understood why, so I kept it hidden from my family and friends. My parents were still very Old World and superstitious, believing that which couldn't be explained was the work of something dark and dreadful. Besides that, you and I both understand how cruel children can be.

"I devoted a large part of my life to it, determined to find its meaning. You have no idea how relieved I was to discover that it was not the sign of something dark and evil, but indeed the opposite. My next mission was to find someone else bearing the gift of the angels. I don't have the ability to see my guardian like you, although I can feel a presence with me at times. It wasn't until a few years ago that I understood the reason for the mark I was given."

I looked at him, my breathing flowing easier into my lungs once again, no longer feeling threatened.

"You see," he continued, noticing my ease. "We all have a role to play. An alliance to form. Mine was never spelled out for me, so I had to seek it out on my own."

He gently took the journal and began leafing through the delicate pages. My eyes widened when he faced an open page in my direction. Three names took up the entire page. Hadrian's name was the first, though for whatever reason, it was crossed out. The next two names gave me chills, for they were bold and dark, as if written in blood, and lacked the black streak striking them out.

The second name was Lucifer.

As I read the name, a chill swept through the room and continued down my back.

The third was a name I knew all too well. A name I tried to avoid for years. I looked down again, the five letters burning themselves into my head.

Brynn.

Chapter Twenty-Seven

"The earth is a footprint of the heavens. It works like a mirror." Nate's voice was pitched with unnerving excitement. Finally, he had found someone to share his secret with and he paced feverishly across the uncluttered sections of the study. "Are you familiar with the trinity?"

I slowly nodded my head. Church had ingrained the trinity in me since I was small.

"Three is a powerful number. There are legends, stories of its sacred power, and I have come to learn that those stories should not be taken lightly."

He made his way over to the tall wall of shelves and earnestly began searching the spines on the lower shelves. If the bookcase was arranged in some sort of order, I would never know. The titles seemed to be placed randomly and only he seemed to know the code. He pulled a small black book from the shelf and thumbed through it.

"The Rule of Three, the karmic law that what you send out comes back to you threefold, or at three times the power under which you sent it out."

He replaced the book and chose another. That one was reddish-brown and ripped, having seen much better days.

"Three, as in the maiden, the maid and the crone . . ."

Another book came down from the shelf and Nate read from its pages, "The number "3" is used many times in Chinese culture. As mentioned in the I Ching, pronounced E Ching. It stands for Heaven, Earth and Man. When we bow to offer incense, it is always done three times. In bonsai and ikebana, the patterns follow an irregular triangle to represent the trinity of heaven, earth and man."

He replaced the last book and looked at me long and hard. "The fallen believe in the power of the trinity as well. In this case, it consists of three names. If you were to double the power each one holds within himself, it is the same as counting the person twice." He pointed to each name and began counting by twos. Two, four, six.

"Now give each one the final number," he instructed me.

"Six, six, six," I whispered.

There was silence as he allowed me to take it all in.

"It is Lucifer's mark. See how he stands between them," his finger pointed to the name in the middle.

"I don't understand. Why is Brynn's name here?"

To me she was a stuck-up girl who harbored a lot of issues. To see her name on this list had me completely confounded.

Dr. Dean's shoulder's dropped. "I'm not sure how she fits in. Somehow she's managed to channel Lucifer's darkness into her own life. Acknowledging his existence has given her some sort of destructive purpose." He moved in closer and cautiously took my hand, exposing my lemniscate. "Do you see the mirror image you hold, Teagan?" He drew a line down the middle of the lemniscate with his finger, splitting it in two lengthwise. For a brief second I could envision it - the eight became a different number altogether. A three.

"It may be impossible to destroy such power but at least you can change it."

I stared back at him puzzled.

"You are the stake to split the darkness. You are the light."

Light. Memories of Garreth filled me.

"To offset the power of the three, you must rely on three of your own. Do you know who I speak of?"

"But Hadrian, he's on this list. How can he help?"

"The opposite of light is dark. Some may think they work against each other, but they don't. In fact that is the only way they can work. To balance."

I thought of Garreth. How could I get a hold of him to even think about helping me? He was practically ignoring me. Except for that look he gave me tonight at the dance. Was the Garreth I knew regaining control?

"As Hadrian has turned away from Lucifer, Garreth has begun to turn away from you. It is the mirror of light and dark. You must reach him in time before he totally succumbs to true human essence."

I nodded. My brooding had been masking how I truly felt about us. I was surprised to realize that everything we had been through, everything we had meant to each other could quickly be pushed aside. He was in my world now and I needed to step up and help him somehow. Once again, I was feeling the bond between us resurface. I missed him so much.

"Teagan," Nate interrupted, "you must go after Brynn. She has no idea what she has done.

"You, and only you, can give her what she seeks. It is the only way to undo what she has started."

"I don't understand. What could she possibly want from me?" I was worried now, but ready to fight for an end to this.

Nate opened the journal about three quarters of the way toward the end and ripped a page from it. The gesture took me off guard. He had gone through great lengths to protect this book and now he was ripping it apart. But with one glance at the page he offered me, I understood why. It was the map. The same map Brynn had stolen earlier this evening.

On it were sketched trees, a whole forest full, and a river at the base of a long, curved line. I took the drawing and studied it, feeling my heart quicken as I recognized a clearing in the middle of all the tiny trees with a small square drawn in the center of it. The shape of a cross had been drawn directly above it.

"There's a ruined chapel in the woods. It was called Saint . . ."

"Saint Anne's," I whispered. "I've been there."

A smile tugged at his mouth.

"You know how to get there then?"

"Yes, of course."

Dr. Dean raked his hands through his messy hair and walked to his desk. "I was going to stay here, in case Brynn came back, but I'll go with you. It's late."

"It's fine. I've been there plenty of times. I'll go and you stay here. You know, in case she comes back."

But his eyes said it all and we both knew how unlikely it was that Brynn would come back here. She had the map, an evil plan, and a very determined mind. And apparently I was the only one who could help her.

Chapter Twenty-Eight

I didn't mind that Nate stayed behind to wait for Brynn. I knew these woods well. Plus there was no way I was going to be chaperoned by my mom's boyfriend just because of some trees in the dark. Although, I had second thoughts when he reinforced the significance and power of my mark, insisting I was the only one strong enough to fight Brynn's demons. But it was only because he said the word demon.

Without a doubt, I knew the small scale drawing on the map was Saint Anne's. It wasn't that hard to recognize. I also understood I wasn't meant to do this alone. So, of course I wrestled with myself emotionally the entire drive, weighing the possibilities if I would find Brynn there, still believing she had discovered something important, and if so, would I find Garreth there as well?

My answer soon came to me, but it wasn't Garreth waiting for me.

It was Hadrian.

His dark silhouette stood tall and still in the clearing as I drove to the end of the narrow path flanked by overgrowth. My heart was pounding. Hadrian had always lured me. Even in the moments when I had genuinely feared him, his soul called to mine. Garreth, on the other hand, was so light and pure. Now more than ever, we needed to lean on each other, but convincing him of that worried me. We had become too estranged these last few weeks.

My eyes scanned the trees closest to the constricted lane. The leaves had been falling for weeks, thinning out the normally dense forest, but from what I could see there was no sign of Brynn's car. That tiny fact made me realize I was alone in the woods with Hadrian and I shivered slightly.

"I'm looking for Brynn," I said, pushing against the door of the car and crunching my way over to him.

Hadrian's dark hair stirred in the breeze and he held his hand out to me, making me feel a bit safer.

"I know, but you'll need help finding her."

Silently, we walked through the dark to where the ruined chapel stood. The last time he and I were here felt eons away. At night, it looked even more deteriorated than the afternoon I had escaped here. Though it was merely a pile of rocks and glass now, it harbored shadows that didn't exist during the day and felt creepier than I thought it would. I was glad I wasn't alone.

I checked the black corners, scanning for Brynn, but she was nowhere, and I looked back at Hadrian, confused.

He reached down and hooked his finger onto a metal ring in one of the large square stone tiles on the floor. I was completely taken by surprise to see that one of those tiles hid a trap door. It appeared to resist as Hadrian pulled on the ring, but finally gave way revealing a small, cramped space leading down to a pitch black hole in the ground.

"This is just the beginning," Hadrian's voice floated across to me in the dark.

"Beginning of what?"

"A journey to overcome my brother's obsession for control over the willing."

"Don't tell me I need my dagger again." I thought of following Brynn the same way I had followed Garreth last spring. The ornate dagger had proved to be a portal and although it had worked, the idea filled me with dread. I had been desperate to find Garreth. I wasn't that desperate to find Brynn.

"No, this time you only need to follow a sacred path, proving you truly believe that light is more powerful than darkness."

Had I heard correctly? Did Hadrian believe light was more powerful than darkness? Thoughts of redemption seeped their way in and I searched his face for the answer, but all too quickly, he turned his attention once again to the dark hole in the floor.

"The tunnel will take us to the river. From there we cross into New Hope and make our way to another old church. I am certain we will find Brynn there." Hadrian's black boot pushed aside some of the rubble lying on the stone floor of the chapel. It had always been littered with stained glass and metal, but the damage was far worse now after the fire last spring. I shuddered with the memory.

I couldn't imagine a tunnel stretching that far beneath our feet. The map didn't show tunnels at all, just trees. Stealing a glance over to my car, I wondered if we could drive there? I had left the map in the car, assuming Brynn would be here. It didn't show anything other than the church.

This church.

"Why are we going to a church that happens to be miles from here?" I tried to catch a glimpse of his face, but it was too dark.

"We are not going to a church. We are going to what lies beneath the church, and it's actually closer than you realize. These tunnels were dug three hundred years ago and the pilgrimage to the sacred ground at the other end had been by foot. We must follow in the same manner."

The number three rang in my ears. I stood staring from Hadrian's shadowed face to the dark hole to nowhere he had just uncovered.

"Long ago, humans blessed the earth their sanctuaries were built on. Not just the buildings themselves. It's the oldest one within walking distance."

"But what about this one? The one we're standing in? Or on rather." I looked around at the ruin. Sadly, not much was left.

"The one waiting for us is older, if you take in account the foundation and the earth it stands on. I'll go first so I can help you down," Hadrian offered, and he began hoisting himself above the opening that would swallow him whole.

I peered inside. "I'm not so sure light is stronger than dark." I shook my head and took a step back. "Um, I am not going down there."

Hadrian's brows furrowed. He was resting his weight on his arms and half his body was already submerged in darkness.

"You can and you will. Now come on."

I leaned over, trying to see past his torso, but I could see absolutely nothing.

"Are you afraid of the dark, Teagan?" he asked, mockingly.

"Maybe."

"But you are not afraid of me?"

I answered him with silence.

"You are a strange girl, indeed, Teagan McNeel," he smirked.

I sighed deeply and grudgingly placed my bottom on the cleanest looking side of the hole I could find. Slowly, I inched myself closer to the edge.

In a blink he was gone, landing lightly onto what I assumed was the floor of the tunnel and the start of our mysterious journey to find Brynn. Meanwhile, I was silently kicking myself for rushing off without a flashlight. I looked down at my mark for reassurance. It seemed subdued and dim with absolutely no sign of warning, or impending danger. For now. I closed my eyes and let myself drop and his strong arms caught me as my eyes adjusted to the darkness of the tunnel. It only took a few moments, but I was reluctant to let go of him. His arms felt protective and strong. For a moment I could pretend I wasn't about to face something even darker and stronger than Hadrian.

He gently put me down and took my hand, pulling me along into an unknown that stretched out like a serpent before us. I jumped as a flash of light struck and Hadrian lit a crude torch with his bare hands. In the light of the flame, I could see the ground had been hollowed out. The walls of the tunnel had been worn down in spots, revealing clay patches throughout the hardened mud. Above us roots and vines protruded through the dirt ceiling. The image of spiders and other creepy, crawly things passed through my thoughts and I wrapped my arms around myself.

"This has always been a sacred journey." Hadrian's voice sounded deep and strange to me as we walked. "Long before the settlers of this town arrived, a small group of people worshipped here. They came from the surrounding territories, walking for miles to get here. Some arrived on horseback, but in the end they, too, continued by foot."

"I would have kept the horse," I muttered to myself.

"It is believed that walking beneath the ground made you one with the earth. Coming out of the tunnel and breathing the fresh air honored the sky above, and crossing the river bed was to remind them of their birth. Finally, at the end of their journey, they lit the fire and celebrated their spirits being set free. It was an honored rite to make this journey, one that made them stronger and closer to the visible and unseen worlds around us."

I tried to imagine multitudes of feet trampling the same ground we were now walking on. I wondered what was at the end of the tunnel. More so, what I would find at the end of our journey.

At last we reached a point where the ground sloped upward. Hadrian went first, still holding my hand, helping me out of the tunnel. We stood at the edge of the river bank for a moment. I was happy to catch my breath as I looked across the black water. Hadrian was right, it was refreshing to take large breaths of air now that we were out of the dank ground. I filled my lungs to capacity and found I couldn't help but stare up at the beautiful sky. I didn't know if this simple act was an act of devotion to the vastness above me, but it did make me feel alive and thankful. Staring at the stars and the thin wisps of cloud tracing across the night sky made me think of all I have been through and seen. And when a brilliant star caught my eye, I thought of Garreth and made a wish that I would find a way to fix things between us.

"Come," Hadrian urged once again. He stepped into the icy water and reached out to help me follow. I didn't complain this time. Forcing myself down a dark hidden hole in the middle of the woods at night seemed far worse than wading across a river. Of course, I tried not to think of the fish and plant life slinking past my legs — or the squishy mud my feet kept sinking into. The water was freezing and I was shivering uncontrollably by the time we battled the current and reached the other side.

Quickly, we made our way up the embankment and through the tall grass to another inconspicuous opening in the ground. I thought for sure retreating beneath the ground with soaking wet clothes and hair would make me feel even colder, if that was possible. But surprisingly, warm air blew invitingly from the opening. This tunnel had a more gradual slope, but from what I could tell, there seemed to be no end in sight. My shoes felt sloshy and disgusting, full of river water and goodness knows what else.

My wet dress was heavy against my legs as we walked, and before long, my feet lost the will to do anything more than shuffle. I reached up, tucking a damp strand of hair behind my ear, and stifled the sigh that had been building deep in my chest. This journey would have been next to impossible without Hadrian. He walked steadily ahead of me, his presence constantly urging me to follow. I honestly had no idea how those people long ago had done it. If I had come alone, I would have plopped down on the ground a good ways back and given up.

As the tunnel leveled out, I could see that the dirt wall had become smoother, and it now reflected an orange glow. The tunnel widened and we slowly crept closer toward an unusual, flickering light.

"It must be the middle of the night now. We've been gone so long." Worry threaded its way through me, and I thought of my mother. Hopefully Nate had called her to explain, although what he could tell her without making her freak out was beyond me. I pulled my cell phone out of my pocket, but there was no service here.

"How far down are we?" Weary and somewhat annoyed, I shook my phone and held it high above my head, willing it to pick up a roaming signal.

"About fifteen feet, give or take." Hadrian's voice was husky and deep as he let his hand glide along the wall, as if feeling the past speak to him through his fingers. I half expected him to stop and press his ear to the dirt and stones, pausing long enough to hear the secrets, but still, we moved along, trudging further beneath the ground. Then I realized the walls were faintly streaked with white.

"What is that? Those marks on the wall?" I asked quietly.

"Salt. The original worshippers believed that by blessing the ground with salt, evil could not cross it."

I wish it was that easy, I thought silently.

Suddenly, Hadrian's arm extended protectively in front of me and we abruptly stopped walking. I studied his face, but he was listening intently. I heard nothing, except the crackling of inviting flames, and my shivering body yearned to keep moving until I was standing in front of the fire I knew was just around the bend.

Slowly, we moved forward as the walls of the tunnel gave way to a large open room, like a stone antechamber. The space had a very old feel to it and I took note of the stones lining the walls around us; how they appeared rugged and inconsistent in their pattern as roots and vines pressed through the spaces within the aged mortar.

A large fire burned in the middle of the floor, its warmth so enticing that I started to walk toward it, eager to thaw my frozen hands and feet and dry my sodden clothing. But Hadrian still held tightly onto my hand, refusing to come with me, keeping his back pressed against the cold wall. It was only then that I heard the sound of movement coming from the opposite side of the fire.

A small figure crouched on the floor, tracing lines in the dirt. She rocked back and forth, humming quietly to herself, oblivious to the fact that we were watching. My heart lurched as she suddenly stopped, rising to her feet. Her bare arms were covered with long scratches, the same lines she had been tracing on the floor. Her hair was messy and her dress was smudged. My hand covered my mouth as she turned, and then I felt a pull. Hadrian was now stepping out from the shadows, and I had no choice but to follow into the light of the bright orange flames.

Chapter Twenty-Nine

The fire went cold.

Sure, I was staring at it, watching the flames curl and extend toward the ceiling of the dank room, but it suddenly felt absent of heat.

My entire body seemed to ice over, and strangely, my thoughts raced back to the unnatural cold I had felt in the closet of Brynn's house. It was cold there when it shouldn't be . . . like here. I felt as if my bones were about to crack, the air was so frigid. Brynn's face was pale and her eyes were closed. Surprisingly, she seemed very small to me. She trembled with an anxiety I couldn't put my finger on. A feeling of absolute terror seized me without warning. There was no sound, no visible reason for me to react this way, only the sight of Brynn stricken by something I wasn't sure I wanted to understand. My legs felt the instinctive urge to run, but they were frozen.

Last spring Hadrian was the darkest obstacle in my world, but this felt worse.

Hadrian released my clammy hand, leaving me alone with my pounding heart.

"What did you do, Brynn?" Hadrian's voice pierced the air. Each word felt like a slice, hard and swift.

Brynn turned her head, but either refused or was unable to answer Hadrian. The tension in the room was horrifying.

"You let him in, didn't you?" Hadrian's voice bellowed and I felt myself shake against my will, no longer just shivering from the cold.

Brynn's hand swept quickly to her mouth, covering it. She opened her eyes and stared at Hadrian.

My God, what could she have done?

His knuckles were clenched as he crossed the floor in three strides and grabbed her by her shoulders, making her look like a tiny, limp doll next to his tall, lurking form. Hadrian could be formidable when he chose to and I could hear the stretching and tearing as his dark wings released themselves from his flesh, eager to expand.

"A bargain?" Hadrian asked, his dark eyes frantically searching hers, yet she still didn't respond. "What did you offer, Brynn? Tell me!"

A high keening was beginning to bounce off the walls, and my arms answered the new sound with gooseflesh. I realized the sound was coming from Brynn. She was falling apart, shaking, whimpering. Her eyes bulged with irrational fear, but she wasn't focused on Hadrian. She was oblivious and lost somewhere inside the depths of her own tortured mind.

"You stupid . . . ," his hand raised in the cold, light of the room, prepared to strike.

"No!" I screamed. My voice echoed and fell. I braced myself against the hatred I would see in his eyes but he turned to me, ridden with agony instead.

"You would save her?" Hadrian shook his head in disbelief. "Don't you see?" He glanced at Brynn for a moment, then slowly faced me again, struggling to gain control of himself. His wings rippled with tension and at last fell silent and still by his side. His eyes were fixed with a sudden realization that confused and frightened me, and then with an ineffable sadness, he whispered, "You're the pawn."

Hadrian let Brynn drop to the ground, shaking in silence, the pieces of herself fallen and lost with the words Hadrian had just set free. In their presence I felt bitterly alone.

The whimpering started again and I wanted to tell her to shut up so I could hear myself think. With feverous speed I tried to make sense of this, but the ideas weren't coming like I wanted them to. They were painfully slow and treaded through my mind like sludge. What was happening? Why was Hadrian staring at me so sadly? Why wouldn't Brynn shut the hell up?

My head hurt horribly and my hands shot up to my hair and my fingers grabbed and pulled. Everything came rushing past the sludge just then.

Too fast.

I desperately wanted to go home, or better yet, have Garreth here to calm me and take this horrible feeling away. But it was just as I had feared it would be in the end. Just me.

A hum circulated through the air. An alien white noise. Buzzing. Hissing. I realized that Hadrian had turned back and was paying close attention to Brynn. She was chanting and rocking back and forth, completely unaware of her audience.

Her arms wrapped tightly around her torso as if holding in the pieces.

"He promised me." The words spilled out of her mouth, splitting the cold silence. I could almost see the room ripple with her voice.

"I could only pick one." Her sentence cut short with laughter. "Could you blame me for picking the better of the two?"

She sounded like such a little girl. Her beautiful pale face looked innocent as she went on about her choices. For all I knew she could have been talking about pairs of shoes or the school lunch menu.

"What was the first choice, Brynn?" Hadrian prompted.

She looked in his direction with unseeing eyes, miles and miles away from the room the three of us were standing in.

"Solitary happiness." She spoke as if we should know what she meant.

"And the second?"

Tears began to roll down her cheeks. For a moment I was stunned. I had never seen Brynn cry before and the sight of it startled me. It was so easy to forget she was human just like me. I felt time slow down and speed up in the same instant. All of a sudden I didn't just know what her answer would be, I felt it.

"She would come back to me." Brynn's mouth formed a tiny smile.

"Who? Who would come back to you?" Hadrian asked, with impatience.

She turned to him, deft awareness returning to her brown eyes.

"My mother," her voice rang with condescending innocence.

At that precise moment, a chill swept through me and I heard a voice far away in my conscience.

Give her what she seeks. Give her what she wants.

The words echoed inside me. It was what Nate had said back in his study.

Through my peripheral vision, I could see the outer spans of the room dimming. Shadow was closing in on us and I began to tremble.

With a ripping snap, Hadrian's wings spread wide open, casting Brynn and me in dark shadow. Panic was in the warm breeze wafting down on us from the fluttering of Hadrian's enormous wingspan. My hand tingled with searing heat and I grabbed my wrist in pain. Never before had I felt my mark blaze with such ferocious warning.

A hissing sound came to my ears through the quickly dimming room. I could see Brynn's lips moving. She was chanting over and over to herself as she rocked back and forth. Her eyes were fixed and glazed.

"Snuff the light . . . snuff the light . . . snuff the light . . ."

Over and over she continued until my head was on the verge of exploding. I looked at my hand. My scrolled mark was shimmering with a white light.

What was happening?

I felt myself being pulled away from reality. Unexpectedly, the present came to a screeching halt, allowing a timeline of events to flash before my eyes. I saw Garreth in my head as he was the day he gave me his white, protective light, the very light that was supposed to save us from Hadrian. I saw Claire standing in the cemetery. I saw Hadrian slamming my father in the chest with a blue light. I saw my mother open the door to my bedroom and smile, but it was Brynn's white sterile room, not mine. I saw Mathur condemning Hadrian to an eternity of misery. Above me, a black octagram swirled clockwise, its eight points blurring as it spun wildly out of control.

My thoughts were muddled as the shadows grew closer. I felt a breeze warm like breath.

I couldn't feel my body and it felt wonderful. All the memories that hurt me throbbed and coursed out of my hand and trickled away. All I had held inside of me, all that was a part of me. . . my heart had been so full and now it was such a relief to feel it empty. I was moments away from losing consciousness and all I could think about was the delicious silence.

I floated in a dark pool marbled with white light that rippled and threatened to disappear. Very slowly, the pain I felt came back in waves, bringing with it the white light, the blinding brightness of reality, for wasn't the absence of color the symbol of death?

If only I could be so lucky.

With the growing light, the pounding in my skull worsened. My body felt fractured in a zillion places and I truly feared I would never feel the same again. Did I dare open my eyes?

I waited for the darkness to return, an emptiness that was so comforting and still, but it refused, and now I could only feel this strange, trembling breeze.

Brynn's wailing had stopped. Maybe she passed out? That would be a good thing, I thought to myself.

Gradually, new thoughts began to trickle through my brain. What did Hadrian mean when he confronted Brynn? Time warped for a moment as I watched him changing . . . his wings, dark and beautiful, how I remembered him from my dreams. He was frightening, but it was who he was.

But Brynn? To feel such a devastating unhappiness. What would make her do something so desperate?

And me?

You're the pawn . . . Hadrian's words stung me now.

I had never trusted Brynn, and yet I still felt betrayed.

My hand hurt. It felt welted and hot, and when I made a fist I felt it on the tips of my fingers. The gentle wind was whispering to me again. I floated to the surface. *How long have I been under? Please . . . I want to stay.* I was unable to remember why I was here or why the beating of my heart sounded so far away.

For a brief moment I remembered someone . . . blonde, blue-eyed . . . he lingered on the edges of my reality, but I couldn't reach him.

My skin prickled. I was almost awake. Knowing flooded my brain and I heard it once again . . .

"snuff the light . . ."
It would not go away and I knew. . .
I am the light of which she speaks.

Chapter Thirty

I cautiously opened my eyes.

My wish for darkness had been granted. It surrounded me . . . wings, arms . . . a feeling of weightlessness. And then a most beautiful face. The face of an angel.

"Hadrian," I whispered.

He seemed relieved that I recognized him.

"That insipid child should know not to play with fire. She has no idea what she's done by opening a gate," he warned, stealing a glance just behind his shoulder.

My eyes must have shown my confusion. I was having trouble snapping into focus.

"Gate?"

"Her desperation let him in and he's the purest form of evil, Teagan. He'll stop at nothing now, ripping away from us all we hold dear. Your mother . . . your friend, Ryan . . . ," he looked away for a moment. "He'll take you away from me."

"What do you mean, she let him in?" My tongue felt thick in my mouth, but with each passing second I was swiftly becoming aware of my strange surroundings — and that I was with Hadrian, whose dark eyes appeared tender.

"She didn't just open a gate to let Lucifer in. She *is* the gate."

I felt a shudder creep down my spine at that. Although I didn't understand the significance, it still seemed obvious that it was a starring role for Brynn. Something important, and horrific at the same time.

"As heaven exists in our minds, so does hell. To someone like Brynn, who has offered herself as a vessel, it is a very strong reality."

"She sees him?"

"In her mind, yes. Lucifer wields his power through emotional thought, much like a guardian."

"He doesn't look like a person? Like you do, and . . ." I was about to say Garreth.

"When Lucifer was cast out of paradise he was stripped of all luxury, including the ability to materialize in the flesh. He renounced his role as a guardian and chose the path of darkness, so in darkness he shall always remain, seeking refuge in the minds of those who allow him in."

"But how do we help her?"

I looked at Brynn with new eyes. The fuse of loathing that would usually ignite faltered. It spluttered and fell silent. She looked back at me and her eyes said so much. We didn't need words. She knew. I knew. We each stretched a little out of our normal zone of comfort and finally, we met in the middle.

I couldn't bring myself to hate her anymore. She was just a girl, like me. My hand tingled and instantly, I knew the endless stream racing through her thoughts; that I could give her something.

Something she would be willing to accept.

Something I was on the brink of being ready to give.

I could see a glistening tear escape and roll down Brynn's cheek. Could there possibly be a way to undo the damage she's started? How she learned of Nate's journal in the first place, I'd never know. She was vindictive and harsh, always seeking a means to destroy and gain. But as I looked back on how she treated my mother, how she was so careful and tentative with her actions, I understood. To Brynn, my mother was a fragile thing that could be broken at any moment. Brynn was trying to recreate one desperate attempt to hold once again what had been ripped away from her. Reason was lost to her the moment her heart broke. She had made a wish . . . and the wrong person heard it.

On unsteady legs, I walked over to her. Clearly, I didn't expect an apology. Brynn had never been the type to give one. I knelt down beside her, still leery of this girl who would go to such lengths to get what she wanted.

"We can't bring your mother back. I'm sorry," I whispered.

Brynn shrugged, then looked away.

"Your father loves my mother. Perhaps . . ." it was the last thing I wanted to offer, but I knew in my heart it could be the beginning she needed. It could be the very thing Nate said only I could give her.

"I didn't know what I was doing!" Brynn cried. "He promised me I would see her again!" Her body practically crumbled, she was shaking fiercely with regret. "I didn't understand."

Hadrian approached quickly. "When did Lucifer make you this promise?"

Brynn sank back to the floor, her entire body drawing in to a tight little bundle. She shook her head violently to and fro.

"Tell me!" Hadrian's voice made the room shake and even I trembled at the enormity of his power.

But Brynn's body went completely still.

Hadrian and I stood staring, waiting, but there was nothing. It was as if someone had just turned off Brynn's switch. Her expression was blank and her tears, which moments before had been flowing freely, now seemed to be frozen on her cheeks. I leaned in, venturing to get a closer look at the girl who had just been freaking out, hoping to get some reaction, but she was a blank canvas. Empty.

"What just happened?" I asked breathlessly.

Hadrian's eyes were still focused on Brynn. "I'm not quite sure."

My eyes darted around the room, but I saw nothing that should cause Brynn's sudden muteness.

With a flash, her eyes closed tight, and she turned her head as if trying to face away from something. Her arms cautiously reached out, slapping at the empty air of the antechamber, then quickly recoiled back to her chest where she crossed them protectively around her. Brynn scooted backwards, her once beautiful dress ripping beyond repair, until her back was flat against the dirt wall, where she whimpered in fear.

"She's struggling, but Lucifer is too strong for her to fight off alone."

"She's fighting him off? That's good, right?" I tore my eyes from the trembling girl before us back to the angel next to me.

"Yes, it's a start. A part of her has come to her senses, and she's attempting to resist him. Having her in this place helps."

Hadrian studied her face, his eyes widening. I took an apprehensive look for myself, worried and fearful.

Brynn's body jerked violently and then shuddered. She opened her mouth and exhaled a breath so deep it sounded as if it would be her last. Her eyes shot open and focused on the ceiling. Hadrian and I stood frozen. The air in front of us shifted, as if the room were breathing on its own. Hadrian's body stiffened, his back poised and ready for the full expansion of his magnificent wings. I moved closer, positioning myself safely at his side, but there was only silence and stillness as Brynn's face transitioned back to a peaceful expression. Her chest now rose and fell at regular intervals and she leaned her head back against the wall. Sweat beaded across her dirty face, but at least she was calm for now.

"Brynn did well," Hadrian's voice broke the silence.

"Well? As in a good job?" I turned and looked back at Brynn and suddenly felt the need to take a step away from them both. All I could think of was how her eyes looked, how her chest sounded when she breathed. How it all began and ended so suddenly like a ticking time bomb; how it could all start over at any given second.

"Yes, it was a start, but Lucifer is allowing his strength to show. Rarely does he manifest himself physically as well as mentally in someone."

"Why Brynn? Why is he attacking her? Tormenting her so violently?"

Hadrian looked at me like the answer was obvious.

"Because she's trying to back out of the deal."

I stared at Hadrian. How could he explain this all so easily; how could he take it all so lightly?

Looking back at Brynn, I could see she was sleeping, at least for now. The crease on her forehead was gone and she looked serene, even after all that had happened. But I shivered inside.

He was there. Waiting. In her mind.

And here.

Waiting in my mind.

Hadrian took a step closer to me, his hand reached for mine, the very hand I had once feared now stretched toward me to comfort me.

"I told you of the journey, of the pilgrimage. The river was not always there. The tunnels connected from church to church, from one sacred point to the other, scattered throughout these parts. There are eight of them."

The significance hit me. I looked down at my hand.

"It was during one year, there was a terrible flood and the river changed course, crushing parts of the tunnel. The water could not erase it from the earth, but only give it new meaning."

"Birth," I whispered.

"Yes, birth. Not human birth, but birth from darkness and evil. A strength to overcome in numbers. This place is holy. Each stone laid with a prayer that still resonates to this day. But it isn't enough," he said with the upmost gravity, "we must guard what we choose to believe."

But I was having trouble believing in anything other than what I had just seen. If Lucifer was in Brynn's mind, then that meant he was in this very room with us. Right now. I was having a moment. My breath was suddenly stuck in my chest. I looked at Hadrian, who was my only anchor in this right now.

"So, if Lucifer is in her mind, then that means he's still here. With us." I watched and trembled as Hadrian nodded slowly confirming my fear.

Then, all my thoughts snowballed at that point. I looked at Brynn. I looked at the fire. If this place was so holy, then why would Lucifer be here?

"How did *Brynn* get here?"

And out from the shadows on the opposite side of the room stepped my still-beautiful guardian, Garreth.

"I brought her."

Chapter Thirty-One

He was like a beacon of light stepping from the dark side of the stone room. He was brilliant and beautiful, and my heart tugged painfully.

Although I was happy to see him, the realization set in once again that I was caught between two angels, and I felt Hadrian tense beside me. He had a cold, almost protective fierceness about him now, while Garreth appeared surprisingly calm, yet significantly changed.

"You brought her?" Hadrian seethed dryly.

"I did."

Hadrian's eyes narrowed, "You came across the water?"

"No, I'm well aware that the full journey can only be made with the help of one's guardian, and I'm not Brynn's guardian." With that, Garreth looked directly at me, confirming what had been nagging at me for so long. That he indeed still cared for me, and that I really did have two guardians.

"And we're supposed to believe you did this, for what? To help Brynn? Out of the goodness of your heart?"

"Hadrian, please." I gave him a look that I hoped would settle him.

"Did you believe I'd forgotten my role as guardian? That I'd abandoned all that I really am?" Garreth asked. Then shifting his focus, he walked slowly toward me. It had been weeks since he'd shown me any type of consideration or concern.

"You needed Brynn where she would be at her weakest. So, here she is." He handed me a curled paper—the map Brynn had stolen from Nate's study, which would have only taken her to the first chapel.

I wanted to cross the space between us and bury myself in his arms, bury the past few weeks that had been miserable without him. But I stood still, my feet planted firmly on the hard dirt floor. He stopped a few feet from me, reluctant to come closer without invitation. I searched his eyes for anything harsh that would otherwise convince me not to trust him, but I only saw the familiar blue that I had feared was lost to me.

Hadrian intervened, stepping between us, his gaze on Garreth.

"You left her unprotected."

"And I see you had no problem stepping in."

I could feel a strange force take shape within the room. Hadrian and Garreth's energies were colliding, and I could immediately sense that, if taken too far, it could be destructive.

"This is not what we're here for! Stop fighting about this!"

But neither angel relaxed nor took his steely gaze off the other.

With Hadrian between us, I was almost afraid to move closer to Garreth. Afraid that if I took one teensy step, it would mean I was once again choosing sides. Was it possible to be neutral? Where exactly did my heart draw the line? Somehow deep inside, I knew the answer to the choice I would soon need to make, no matter how painful that choice was.

We silently assessed each other, standing still as the fire crackled away. A slight motion shifted our attention, and I could now see that Brynn was beginning to stir. Hadrian was the first to move closer, checking her pulse, examining her pupils beneath her weary, transparent eyelids. But as he stood and faced me, the look in his eyes made me fear Brynn was not making any sort of recovery yet. She was pale with deep circles beneath her eyes and looked extremely weak. In fact, I was beginning to think the worst. Perhaps she couldn't fight this, even with our help.

With heavy doubt, I knew Nate's instructions were not going to be easy. Even with the three of us working together to stand up against Lucifer, to push back whatever darkness Brynn had invited in, we would have to work extremely hard.

"Where do we start?" This was all so confusing to me. I had pictured a fight against Lucifer similar to the fight against Hadrian last year in the woods. That there would be flesh to flesh combat, that we would have to outwit each other, that perhaps one or even all of us wouldn't make it. I looked at my hand and mentally split the eight in half. I pictured a three, hoping to draw strength from the fact that it symbolized us, right here and now. I knew we were up against the purest form of evil. Perhaps one that couldn't even be destroyed.

Looking back and forth from Hadrian to Garreth, I tried to connect what we had to work with. Hadrian was dark and strong. Garreth was pure and comforting.

And me? I was the glue. Supposedly, I was the light. The stake.

The pawn.

Hadrian's confrontation with Brynn rang through my head.

I had to let Lucifer in.

As if I had been speaking aloud, Garreth and Hadrian's heads simultaneously turned sharply in my direction, knowing my thoughts instantly.

They both began protesting in unison, their voices growing, bouncing off the stones until I felt dizzy and screamed for them to stop.

"Enough!" Sternly, I looked them both in the eyes.

Garreth spoke first, cautiously, however, as he seemed to realize his absence and distance from me was not entirely forgiven.

"This isn't the same, Teagan. You were lucky you were able to cross over to save me, but this is in no way the same. You can't."

I turned to Hadrian. Moments ago he had plenty to say, but now . . .

"For once, I agree with him," he finally chimed in.

His dark, green eyes locked with mine. I could feel the change in the air immediately. It was calmer, lighter.

"You are an unexplainable radiance to me in a world where I have known only shadows. I couldn't help but want to be near you. I came back because of you." Then peering over my shoulder, Hadrian asked, "Why do you think Garreth risked so much, changing into flesh and blood just to be with you? You are remarkable. You are not a guardian, yet you have protected like one, and you are more than human as well. The explanations simply evade us all."

He paused then, as if feeling the impact of his own words.

"I do know that there is a prophecy of a light coming to break the darkness. The story is very old and now your hand, your mark, tells of its truth."

Very gently, Hadrian pulled me closer to him and rested his forehead on mine, "You are this magnificent illumination."

It was so easy for him to take my breath away, and it didn't even phase me that Garreth was witnessing this moment between us.

"The answer cannot simply be given to you, for it is so much more than any of us realize. Somehow you must draw Lucifer away from Brynn."

"But how will I know? When?" I whispered back.

"No time better than the present." But Hadrian's eyes held something even he didn't wish to acknowledge. Reluctance, maybe?

Immediately, Garreth sprung forward. "You're sending her to the lion's den!"

Hadrian looked up. "Do you have a better plan?" he replied flatly. "Brynn's obviously not strong enough to do it alone."

He turned back to me. "This is about second chances. You gave me a second chance. You saw through the lie I believed in for so long." Hadrian glanced coldly at Garreth. "I like it no more than he does, but if you don't do it, Lucifer will win." He paused. "And I'm willing to help you."

His pledge seemed to stop Garreth in his tracks as he realized that the three of us needed to work together. Would I be willing to give him a second chance as well?

I stared down at Brynn. Her eyes were open, yet unseeing, and every couple of minutes her body would shake with tremors. Time was crucial now.

I held out my hand and in turn, my two angels gave me their hands, our marks united. A burning sensation seared through my skin.

It was time.

Chapter Thirty-Two

"It's not the same; remember that," Garreth's face was a mask. He wore the concentrated resolve well, but I knew worry and fear bled through the strength he was determined to give me. He sighed deeply, afraid for me. For all of us.

"You aren't leaving and going to another realm."

I nodded my head, understanding.

"Lucifer will challenge you. He will do whatever it takes to keep control." Hadrian's voice came to my other ear. "We're right here. We won't leave your side."

If I admitted fear, then I would be weak against Lucifer. Against the dark.

Compassion broke through Garreth's worry, "You'll have to show him a weakness, Teagan. It's how he enters."

Hadrian squeezed my hand gently. "Ready?"

I couldn't answer for fear the strength I was trying so hard to build up would desert me. I entertained thoughts of running from this place, of taking off down the long, twisting tunnels until I came to the river. Surely then my cell phone would pick up again, and I could call my mother to come get me. I could call Nate. I could call Ryan. Anyone. I could find a road, and perhaps a car would come along, and I could beg them to take me home, and I'd wake up to find this has all been a horrible, horrible dream.

Still holding hands, we walked over to Brynn, where I slowly crouched to the floor beside her. They guided me backwards, my head next to hers, my body stretching out in the opposite direction. I reached down, feeling for the filmy fabric of my now stained dress, wanting to cover myself as much as possible against the biting cold of the damp dirt floor. I felt hands do the work for me, then felt my legs being covered with a softer warmth than that of the ruined party dress. I lifted my chin and peered down at my feet to find Garreth gently rubbing my ankles, warming me, soothing me. Shakily, I smiled a thank you, but I was so chilled, it may not have appeared very grateful.

"If anything happens, we're right here." Hadrian looked fierce in the glow of the fire, but it was a look of determination. The face of a warrior. Of a guardian.

Turning my head to glance at Brynn, I could see her eyes were still fixed on the ceiling. Unseeing, yet seeing everything. I wondered where she was right now, deep inside herself. Was she battling the demon who had promised her she would have her mother again? Was she reliving nightmares? Was she happy with more false promises?

I turned my head back and closed my eyes, steeling myself, knowing I had to let him in. Slowly, I began to empty my mind, allowing tendrils of thoughts into my subconscious. Each thought, each fear, was like a whisper, a thread of smoke that wove through my head, snaking around to find the precise point where I could allow it to fester and take shape; to give it permission to become real. I pictured everything that tempted me, hoping it would draw Lucifer closer.

Desperately, I wanted to retreat deeper inside the safety of myself, to be away from the thoughts, the memories, but I allowed them to come full force. I felt a presence near me. Not on the outside of my body, where I knew Hadrian and Garreth were keeping a close watch on me, but here — within me. It was sharing the same space, and so I continued . . .

I felt over and over again the fear of being in the closet with Ryan. I pictured hell all around me, bidding it to come out of hiding and find me. I made myself hear Brynn and her years of taunting, of making me feel worthless and shameful for even being on the same planet as her. And then . . . I made contact, and someone, something, broke through and touched me.

I was standing, though not really.

I looked down at my arm where I had felt a cold hand resting. There was nothing. Then I realized, this was all in my head. Like a dream. A fearful role playing.

It was misty and gray all around me. Cold. I could see a figure shrouded in shadow, moving closer. Was it the one I felt? It moved, creeping closer, until I could finally make out a shape familiar to me. It was Brynn, no longer lying on the dirt floor, but here with me.

"What are you doing here?" she whispered, looking around nervously. She seemed desperate to run to me, but held back, afraid.

Her face was streaked with dirt and dried tears. Her luxurious hair was in tangles. I was taken aback by the way she wrung her hands fretfully.

I pulled myself away from staring at her and tried to take a good look around. It would be easy to answer *I have no idea*, but of course I couldn't say that. Not if I planned on doing anything worthwhile.

"I came to get you out of here." It was the best I could do.

"Where exactly are we, Teagan?" Brynn's voice had an unfamiliar pitch to it. She was scared.

"It's complicated. Let's just get you somewhere safe, alright?" I wanted to get as close as I could to her. Somehow I would need to imagine myself pulling her out of here, and then Garreth and Hadrian would take it from there.

Her breathing was raspy and before I knew it, Brynn was clinging to my arm, looking all around us.

"Where do we go? Teagan, I've been searching and searching. There's no way out of here."

Before I could explain it wasn't an ordinary exit we were about to go through, I felt her knuckles clench my arm painfully. If Brynn could've hidden inside me at that moment, she would have. Her face drained of all color. "He's here. Oh, Teagan, please hurry!"

"Where?" I was wasting time asking that question, forgetting Hadrian had told me I wouldn't be able to see him.

"He's furious with me! Teagan!"

I felt her body shudder against me, and soon began to feel her weight slinking to the floor, pulling me with her. Slashes appeared on her skin in random strokes. Instinctively, I pulled away from her, my eyes refusing to believe what they were seeing.

Suddenly Brynn stood up and stared directly into my eyes. She let out a guttural scream and lunged for my face. "You killed her! You took her away from me!"

I fell back, the force of her striking against me was beyond powerful. There was no way a girl of her build could shove like that, not even for the last pair of shoes at the mall.

"Brynn! What are you doing? Stop!" I tried pushing her off me, but she kept lashing at me with her nails. I knew it was a trick. It was another game Lucifer was playing with our minds. I couldn't imagine what she must be seeing, she was reacting so violently.

Then suddenly, her face lost its contorted shape and her eyes grew less venomous. She was slowly beginning to calm down. I took careful advantage of the little window of opportunity and spoke gently to her, reassuring her she was safe.

"Brynn, stop. It's okay."

I tried rubbing her arms soothingly, even though she could scratch my eyes out at this distance if she lost control again. "You need to focus if we're going to get out of here."

She allowed me to lead her a few steps. We weren't really headed anywhere, but the slightest of steps to me was progress. She was exhausted, so I sat down with her in a protective little huddle. Maybe sleep would come to her, allowing her to finally rest. If she was out for a little, then it would be easier for me to concentrate on getting us back to the stone room beneath the church; back to the two angels waiting for me. I wanted to shut my eyes with her, just for a little while, but her body began shuddering again, and when I looked over at her to try and comfort her, I saw her eyes roll back behind her lids. There was a pulling sensation on my arms. *No, Brynn. Go to sleep.* Then the fear settled in.

Maybe Lucifer was back.

Someone was dragging me to my feet. I opened my eyes, preparing for another hit or scratch to the face, but found I was opening them to the most beautiful scene I could possibly imagine. I saw two pairs of eyes. One blue. One green. Somehow, we had made it back to my guardians.

Quickly I turned, reaching for Brynn. Did I manage to bring her back with me? She was curled up, sleeping soundly beside the fire, color slowly but surely returning to her cheeks.

I reached up to touch the face of the angel closest to me, but the exquisite faces blurred and began to melt together. A black filmy smoke filled the room, and then without warning, I spiraled downward.

Chapter Thirty-Three

I was no longer looking at Garreth and Hadrian but found myself back in the dirt crawl space I had just escaped from. I decided to venture out into the tunnel, wondering if it was the same one Hadrian and I had walked through hours ago. The walls had that same scraped appearance to them I had taken notice of earlier. And then it hit me. How long had I been underground? Was it morning yet? My feet kept walking, as if begging to be led out of this damp, grubby trap. Then I stopped.

"Teagan?"

There was a voice echoing from the other end of the passageway, the very direction I was walking toward.

"Teagan?"

It was my mother.

I broke into a jog. A run would have been more efficient, but I was so weary and the ground was so uneven. A faint glow warmed the packed earth of the tunnel wall a few yards ahead, and I kept my eye on it, pushing myself onward to reach it. When I saw her, I couldn't help but crash into her. I wrapped my arms around her waist and buried my head into her neck, only . . . it was not my mother. The figure I clutched was not warm and tender like a real person. Instead it was strangely chilled and vaporous in spots, formed to serve a momentary purpose.

The image my heart wanted so desperately to see was just one of Lucifer's many tricks, and I had to remember not to want anything while still trapped down here. If I did, it would be presented to me, it would tempt me to reach out and take it, believing in a lie. This was all part of Lucifer's game. This was how he played, preying on the wants of others. He was the deliverer, and by the time you realized it wasn't real, it was too late. But how do you tell yourself not to want? Especially when you're faced with desperation and fear?

Was that what happened to Brynn? Was she so desperate for her own mother that she believed the lie enough to fall deeper into the clutches of something she couldn't control?

But it was too late. The moment I thought of my mother, the very second my heart *wished* for her—that was enough for Lucifer to make his move. The image that was my mom rippled a bit, and then her sweet smile morphed into a sneer, and her face became Brynn's. Her laughter bounced off the walls. I backed away as Brynn's chortle melted into Claire's scream, and as I watched helplessly, the face changed from one to the other and back again. The faces and voices switched back and forth so rapidly, I needed to cover my ears with my hands and turn away.

It was at that moment I began to notice the tiny little bites at my ankles and legs. I looked down, letting out a breathy yelp. Swarming at my feet were tiny, hideous creatures. I swatted at them, hearing their soft little bodies smash into the ground. Horrified and repulsed, I turned and ran the other way.

The ceiling of the tunnel sprang to life. Once a gnarled mess of roots and vines, it was now a tangle of human limbs. Arms and hands extended downward, hands outstretched, clasping and grabbing. They were inches from touching my hair as I fled past them. Is this what hell was like? One horrible mental torture after the next?

Beyond the reach of the dangling arms, I found myself pausing reluctantly to catch my breath. I leaned over, my hands resting on bent knees as my lungs rejected the air I was trying to stuff into them. But there was no rest for me. I was being followed. I turned to see the opaque wall of black rushing toward me seconds before it slammed me into the nearest wall.

The darkness, the hatred, rained down on me. I felt heat burning my skin from the black smoke that wove it's tendrils around my arms, my neck, my legs. Inside, my entire being was a concoction of everything I had ever feared and hated, all wrapped up into one emotion. It seeped deep within, hemorrhaging, to all the spaces inside me.

Lucifer.

I couldn't see him. I questioned if he was even real, if I indeed was in his presence. But I knew the answer to that. No one else could cause these emotions to spread within me.

How would I ever reach my guardians now? Even if I did, Lucifer would never let me go, at least not without pulling them both into this with me.

I felt hatred stirring inside me. I felt hatred toward Nate for coming into our lives. Hatred toward my father for leaving us. I even hated Claire right now for dying on me, and Garreth for leaving me alone. I hated Hadrian's dark beauty, for the way he loved me, and the way I wanted him to. And most of all, I hated myself for wanting both of them.

A tingling touched the very back of my brain. A part of me was still untouched, unchanged. I remembered when Garreth had told me guardians could tap into a person's subconscious. I thought of Ryan. I could hear his voice the night we were in the closet. He was going on about hell being a part of our minds — to think of it was to succumb to it. All the stories of good winning over evil — was it possible? If we learned to tap into the light we each held inside ourselves, perhaps it would block the darkness always yearning to touch us, the evil that was forever seeking a way in. There had to be some sort of balance.

A glimmer of hope hit me just then. My balance was waiting for me just on the other side. It was dark and it was light, and to succeed in banishing evil, I had to acknowledge both. Not run away from one, while chasing the other. It was here all along. The ingredients to the mix. Light and dark.

I struggled to follow Ryan's rule, the one he claimed to be his reason for seeing Claire months after her death. *He simply thought of her.* With that one thought I began to envision Garreth, and my mind filled with light, and when thoughts of Hadrian slowly penetrated my mind as well, I didn't fight it. I allowed them in. There was no guilt, just clarity. But I felt

Lucifer, still clinging to me, refusing to let me go and as soon as my mind unwillingly accepted that he was still here, I felt the sharp claws of the shape he was possessing dig into my back. Thoughts of where I was seemed impossible to block out.

Lucifer. He was fear. He was torment.

His voice struggled against the barrier I was placing. His wrath was venomous, but little by little, I reclaimed what was mine. I looked around to make sure that Brynn had made it out of this fabricated hell and then raised my hand and felt another grabbing hold of it.

It was warm.

It was almost human.

I was closer now, but the claws dug into my legs from below. He wasn't going to let go. He would follow me if he had to. Suddenly there was someone else down here with me, and my eyes adjusted to the figure next to me. Hadrian.

"Go back," I pleaded through gritted teeth. Did I bring him into this?

Hadrian's eyes took me in. "It's almost finished, Teagan," he said nodding. "You need my help." He was more than ready to turn and face the wrath swarming uncontrollably behind me.

"Hadrian, no!" I pleaded again. An ear-splitting, guttural sound escaped the fury behind us. I had been so close to ridding myself of Lucifer by the manner of sheer thought, or lack of it, only now I was distracted. I could only think of Hadrian's safety and by doing so, I could feel Lucifer gaining strength against me again.

"He is my brother. This is as much my battle as it is yours," Hadrian argued, and I could see the desire for bloodshed in his eyes, the need for chaos surfacing once again. "Listen to me, I understand your fears. I have helped create them. It's only right that I help destroy them." He grabbed my hand, turning it over until the lemniscate faced upright, glowing brightly.

"Hadrian, don't look at him. Don't turn around, please. Please stay with me. I can do this." I clung to him, holding him to me. "These are my fears, my hell. Thinking of you just now was an accident. You're not supposed to be here." I searched the determined look in his eyes, begging him to fade from here and leave me. "I'm the light, remember?"

Suddenly, I knew Hadrian's intentions and panic rose within me.

"And I have chosen to protect that light, no matter what the cost." Hadrian pulled me to him, holding me close. His eyes, beautiful and vibrant green, captured me, memorizing me. His lips found mine, and in that kiss, I gave him more of myself than I had ever given him. I gave him a part of my heart.

He pulled away slowly.

"He's waiting for you." His head nodded upward, pointing in the direction of reality. My lifeline.

No! I wouldn't think of Garreth! I won't drag him into this!

"Hadrian . . ."

His eyes stopped me, and he traced his finger along the curve in my hand. "Infinity. That's how long I will protect you." Before I could find the words to argue, his emerald eyes shifted, becoming sheer obsidian. He turned from me, facing the horror behind us.

Desperately, I tried not to listen to the battle at my back. I could hear the snap of bone, the slamming of bodies, and the worst sound of all, laughter. I couldn't bring myself to think of who had released it. Listening was agonizing as the sounds of hell continued to pierce my ears.

Against my will, my body began to shake and tremble with rage, and an intense, white light appeared, streaming from my hand, illuminating the entire chamber, obliterating the shadows.

I spun around to face the demon that was Lucifer. His wings, black and ancient, stretched wide and a sooty substance fell from them as he inched his way closer to me. His head was enormous and sat on top of a gray, hairless body, rippling with muscle. With every movement of his great wings, the smell of rotting flesh was released, nauseating me. His voice was that of a growl, low and vulgar, and he reached out to me. I knew better than to look into his eyes and was thankful for the brilliant light escaping me.

And with Hadrian's sacrifice, I grew stronger.

I shut myself to the idea that a vicious destruction was taking place and concentrated on controlling my fear. The lemniscate in my hand glowed with blinding intensity, but I forced myself to focus on it and nothing else, anchoring myself to the mark that was mine.

I had been blessed with the mark of unity in Garreth's presence, only to have it change to one symbolizing infinity in Hadrian's. My original mark standing for the three of us had evolved into one that meant infinity, uniting us forever.

With each tortured sound that came to my ears, another brick was added to my wall until finally, I had surrounded myself with a barrier strong enough to keep the darkness at bay.

I knew they were gone. I could feel it, but I still couldn't bring myself to really look. A smooth pale hand reached down for me, and I accepted it, feeling it pull me into a blanket of warmth and light. Out of the corner of my eye, I stole a glance, seeing that Lucifer was indeed gone and caught a glimpse of what was left of Hadrian's once magnificent wings.

Chapter Thirty-Four

Garreth wrapped me in warm arms as I stared into what was left of the fire, watching as the last of the embers smoldered, refusing to die to ash. He helped me to my feet, allowing me to lean my weight against him. I should have felt overwrought after what I had just gone through, but mixed with the shock was an undeniable sense of tranquility. A tranquility only Garreth could muster for my sake, and it felt good to be in his arms again. It felt like home.

I wanted to ask if Hadrian was really gone. Would Garreth know for sure? I looked up at his face, and let the question slip away. If Garreth was comforting me, dulling my senses, then he had good cause to.

Together we shuffled toward the mouth of the tunnel. Brynn stood waiting for us, biting on dirty fingernails, looking forlorn and confused. Surely she was ready to get out of her underground mental torture chamber. We guided her gently along the passageway toward the fresh air that awaited us. I looked up, noticing the roots and leaves dangling above our heads as we walked. They were no longer alive and writhing. Numbly, I felt myself being taken along, walking, stumbling . . .

until at last the cool breath of dawn kissed my face, and I knew we were safe.

The sun was just beginning to rise, stirring to life the sounds of the little town. I could hear a car pass, shortly followed by a second, and the rattle of the bridge connecting Pennsylvania to New Jersey across the river that no longer appeared as black as the night before. We followed the sounds, trekking silently through cool, green grass laden with dew to the front of the church we had spent hours beneath. The church was pretty. Gray with black shutters and stained glass windows arching severely toward its roofline. I pictured the pews filled with smiling worshippers, imagined it filled with soothing music, and sighed, thinking of the ordeal we had endured under its foundation.

A few yards up I recognized the sun-kissed glimmer of Garreth's Jeep, but I wasn't prepared for the intense feeling of security the sight of it brought me. I could hear Brynn gently slide the keyboard of her phone closed as we slowly walked to his car. Her grip on reality seemed to be surfacing and I briefly wondered who she had texted. Would her friends even answer her? But nearly ten minutes went by without a single chime back.

When the car pulled up and my frantic mother emerged, followed by a relieved and still disheveled Nate, I realized the numbness was wearing off and that Brynn had arranged our pickup. I could feel the magnitude of all that had happened. My bones hurt. My head ached. I let my mom cradle me, feeling her warmth. Her real warmth. It was her, not an illusion, and I hugged back, realizing I might be squeezing too hard despite my exhaustion and soreness. But she didn't seem to mind.

"Sweetie," her eyes took in our torn and dirty clothes and she immediately went into mom mode.

"What happened to you two?" My mom stared at me, then turned her eyes to Garreth, her voice tender but resonating insistence, especially after noticing how shaken Brynn appeared.

"Um," I looked over at Nate. Suddenly I was at a loss for words.

"I knew you would find her." Then he turned to my mother, "You see, this used to be Mary's church. She would worship here occasionally, bringing Brynn along with her. It only made sense that Brynn would come here to feel closer to her mother on the anniversary of her death. Of course, coming here at night isn't such a good idea, but at least they're safe and sound."

He shot a knowing glance my way, making sure only my eyes saw the grateful thank you behind it. I could sense that he understood all too well everything that had taken place during the night. Of course, I would have to tell him in detail, but that could wait for later. He would want to write it all down in the journal for safe keeping. Maybe he would even give me the honor of drawing the black line through Lucifer's name.

"Garreth took care of me, Mom. I'm okay." But I let her hover and fret. I was too tired to protest.

"Actually," Garreth's voice rose above my mother's worrying. "Teagan took care of us. All of us." His angelic blue eyes included Brynn, then met mine. His voice sounded calm and soothing again, not like the boy I had seen at school these past few weeks, and I hoped we'd found our way back to each other. But his statement sank deeply into my heart. *'All of us.'* No, not all of us. There was one I *couldn't* save. As happy as I was to be alive, I was suffering. A part of me was gone.

Out of the corner of my eye, I saw Brynn and Nate reuniting in quiet. I saw Nate pull her into a hug and that she let him. There was forgiveness in the way he tilted his head and somehow I knew they had finally met half way, accepting each other.

"Let's get home. You three have been out all night and you're a mess." My mother was back to her old self, taking charge, wanting to care for us. I realized the distance that had been growing between us wasn't just my inability to confide in her. It was a reserved way of protecting her. Of keeping her from knowing of matters that didn't belong to our world. I also needed the distance to prepare myself, to face the greatest of fears lurking inside me. It was also up to me to take care of things. But I wondered, *did* I take care of things? Was Lucifer really gone?

And if so, for how long?

Nate held the car door open for my mom while she inarguably announced that hot showers, soup and tea were in order as soon as we reached home. I spied Brynn standing at the curb

229

a few feet away, staring at the church. When she felt my eyes on her, she silently found her way over to me.

"Teagan, I . . . I don't know what to say," she whispered. "The last few hours are a blur to me, but I have a feeling it has to do with that stupid spell I tried at home. I'm really sorry if I hurt you."

She had tears in her eyes again. Did I blame her for her actions? I couldn't possibly. During the short time we were trapped together, I contemplated her actions while she slept. Faced with a similar turn of events, my life would have been just as upside down as hers, although stooping to make a deal with the likes of Lucifer was certainly not the wisest of choices.

"You're forgiven." As soon as I whispered it back, I could feel the weight of guilt slip from her shoulders and cautiously, she reached for my hand and gave it a squeeze before sliding onto the back seat of Nate's car.

"I'll meet you at home, Mom. I'd like to go with Garreth." I was certain she would argue, having not known my whereabouts for an entire night, but she only smiled gently and nodded.

The sweet scent of incense enveloped me the moment I climbed into the Jeep, but even as it tried to comfort me, I couldn't help relive the horror in my head. I traced the lemniscate on my hand over and over, thinking of something I could have done to save Hadrian, but there was nothing. Hadrian knew I could help him become the guardian he was meant to be, and that I would be his undoing.

'My unfortunate fate.'

I could feel Garreth's warm gaze on me as he started the car and I quietly turned my head to meet it. He reached over and guided my head onto his shoulder, letting me rest. His scent was soothing and calming and I breathed in its effect. Sighing, I let the tension and fear I had harbored flood out of me – knowing that it was his way of gradually helping me heal. I smiled into his shoulder. In the days that would follow, we would all heal, and in time, everything would be all right.

Chapter Thirty-Five

I t was Monday and the final bell had already hummed its warning throughout the building. I was still fuddling with the combination on my locker when I felt a warm body slide up next to me.

"So, you're okay?"

I looked over to see Ryan leaning against the neighboring locker and was happy to see the last of his bruises were completely gone. He still had dark circles beneath his eyes, but the evidence of his rocky ordeal these last few months was long gone, at least on the outside.

"Ryan, it's been two weeks," I playfully rolled my eyes and yanked hard on the metal lever.

"You ask me this every day."

He chuckled, sliding his backpack higher onto his shoulder. "I can't help it. You had me worried." Ryan paused, staring out into the hallway for half a second. "But you are okay, aren't you?"

"Yes," I insisted. "I'm fine." He was never going to forgive me for dropping him off after the dance and battling evil without him. A cold shiver went down my back at the thought. What if he had gone with me? Ryan may never have made it out of there. The fears he stored in his mind were permanent and left marks of their existence. Still, I had called him the Sunday after, to fill him in. Actually, I would have called him Saturday, but I slept the entire day.

"So what's the news?"

"My aunt is officially my guardian. Social Services called first thing this morning," he said with a grin.

"Ryan, that's great! Your aunt seems really nice; you'll be in good hands." I let out an involuntary chuckle.

"What's so funny?"

Clearly, he was overlooking the irony.

"Well, it's just that when I lost my guardian angel, you stood in; now it seems you're being rewarded with your own."

"Yeah, she's already feeling comfortable in her new role. She made me homemade biscuits and canadian bacon at the crack of dawn this morning. And my laundry is always folded on my bed. Weird."

He was already reveling in his new life and deserved to be taken care of. I could only hope the years of abuse would become a bad dream of the past.

"You know," he whispered, leaning in closer as I shut my locker for the day. "She even hugs me. For no reason. Just because."

"You need lots of hugs, Ryan. Hugs are good for you."

Ryan smiled, agreeing. He wouldn't admit it out loud, but he knew it too.

"So, Garreth is back, huh?" I followed his eyes down the hall to see my blonde-haired angel making long strides toward us.

"He is."

"And . . . Hadrian?"

I looked down at my shoe and bit my lip, feeling an unexpected catch in my throat.

"Sorry, Teagan, I know what you went through must have been hard."

I looked up into his eyes just as Garreth was upon us and nodded.

"Back to normal, right?" Garreth said softly while flashing a smile at Ryan. Once upon a time, they would have been enemies, but not today.

"I'm still getting used to *normal*." Ryan turned to me. "Just so you know, I'm still keeping my day job. Can't give it up yet. Catch up with you later, Tea. See you, Garreth."

I watched my friend walk away to his next class. It was nice to finally acknowledge that. *My friend.*

Garreth looked at me curiously. "Day job?"

"You may have competition; he's the best watch dog around," I said with a smile. "I just think he's afraid of losing me, like he did Claire."

Garreth understandingly slipped his warm hand into mine.

"So how did you make out on the calculus test?"

"Can you believe I aced it? I didn't even study. Actually this morning, I didn't even remember that I had a test today."

A smile spread across Garreth's perfectly angular face. "See, now you're the one with infinite knowledge."

We rounded the corner past the locker quad at the far end the hall, when Brynn came barreling into the two of us. She was giddy and bubbly.

"Did you see it? It's huge and perfect! I got to help pick it out!"

Scores of fellow students were walking past and lingered around to hear more. Number one, seeing Brynn excited was unusual. Seeing her share that excitement with me was mind blowing.

"I did, actually. You did an amazing job; it's breathtaking." I was trying to ignore the crowd of rubberneckers, especially the three standing against the water fountain. Brynn completely brushed off the fact that not only was she making a spectacle in front of half the student body, but she wasn't sharing her juicy news with her old friends at all.

Sage, Lauren and Emily's eyes widened in the same high, disbelieving arc, but neither came over to ask what the commotion was about. That's alright. Let them wonder. After all, a rumor is more fun to spread when you don't have the story straight.

"Okay, so you're coming over today, right?" Brynn's arm linked through mine as Garreth and I began our trek out to the parking lot.

"Yeah, sure. You're getting a baking lesson, right?"

Brynn's face lit up as she thought about the afternoon ahead. "She's going to teach me how to make those lemon bars of hers."

My mouth couldn't help watering at the thought of my mother's lemon bars. It was heaven in a little yellow square when you bit into one of those. I could just picture the happiness oozing out of my mom's entire being knowing that Brynn was genuinely interested in learning how to bake one of her top secret recipes. I quietly calculated the lesson in my head. With Brynn and my mom in the kitchen, that would give me approximately twenty minutes to speak with Nate. As Brynn was excited about the time she was going to spend with my mom making a delectable dessert, I was equally looking forward to Nate finally showing me the contents of his ever-secretive journal.

"You know," Brynn paused, eyeing the two of us. "You really are good for each other." Then she bounded off, waving goodbye.

"Hellooo—earth to Teagan." Garreth stopped me and took my face in his hands.

"Oh, sorry, just thinking."

"It's a lot isn't it?"

"Overwhelming."

"The fact that your mother has agreed to marry Dr. Dean, or the fact that he's about to share some information?"

"Both, I guess. You know he's been filling her in, little by little. He's shown her the journal."

His Jeep Wrangler was a few parking spaces away, and for some reason, I couldn't get there fast enough.

"Surprisingly, she's okay with it all," I offered. "I wasn't sure how she would handle it, but she says a lot of things that happened make sense now. Nate has a way of explaining that she's always admired."

"Hmm." His reflection on what I had just said took me off guard.

"What?"

"It's just that there's a lot of irony going around today."

"What do you mean?" I turned in my seat, facing him, grateful that the end of the school day madness was shut out by the window.

"Well, Ryan and his aunt. There's a guardian role being played out there." He paused at my raised eyebrows. I had almost forgotten that he knew everything, even conversations he wasn't present for. Garreth would always be witness to everything I said or did.

"Then," he continued, "there's the matter of your mother. She's accepting the impossible in order to close a door that will in essence, open another. While you are taking on every aspect of that closed door and reopening it to find a new future."

I let it sink in.

There were no more secrets. My mother knew. She knew about Garreth being my guardian; she knew about my mark. Suddenly, I couldn't have felt more relieved.

Brynn buzzed around her kitchen like a little bee, stopping to check the list of ingredients my mother had given her ahead of time. Muttering to herself, she checked the temperature on the oven, "350 degrees, preheating. Check. Oh!" She opened the wide utensil drawer in the center island and pulled out a stainless steel can opener, then recounted the cans of lemon pie filling.

"You can bring boxes over anytime, you know. My room's big enough to store them." Brynn was determined to have us packed and moved in, even though it will still be a couple of weeks yet before my mom contacts a real estate agent for our house.

"I thought we were going to wait until after graduation to start packing."

"I just like to be on top of things, that's all," and she continued fluttering about. Seeing this new side to Brynn made my head spin. Never mind the fact that she and I both had major finals to study for, and were getting the last of our college applications in the mail. On top of all that, we had graduation to look forward to. But if Brynn had it her way, my house would be sold, my mom and I moved in, and our parents happily married within a month's time.

"You just want to have a say in the wedding plans, don't you?" I asked a bit absentmindedly as I stared out the window for my mother's car. I was anxious to speak with my future stepfather.

"Who me?" Brynn acted all innocent.

"Of course you! This is a party on the grandest of scales and you're dying to be involved."

"Well, maybe a little."

At last I could hear the tiny pebbles crunching as my mom's car pulled around to the back of the house. Simultaneously, Nate came padding down the hall from his study to greet her. I was nearly bouncing out of my seat.

"Hey, sweeties," she said to Brynn and me; then she and Nate locked in an embrace that had both of us rolling our eyes.

"Well, I see you're all ready for me, Brynn."

"Yep, I have everything you told me to get." She was all smiles, eager for some one-on-one time with the "cure" that would begin to fill the hole in her heart.

"Calculus test went okay?" she aimed at me, not forgetting to include daughter number one.

"Um, yeah. I got an A."

"Well, ladies," Nate found the opportune moment to interrupt. "You two better get baking. I've been salivating for these lemon bars for about a week now."

Without any further discussion, my mother and Brynn set to work, and Nate wiggled his index finger for me to follow.

My feet knew the way to the study. I could find it with my eyes closed now if I had to. Once past the massive walnut door, he motioned for me to come sit on the settee. A roaring fire was already in the fireplace, and a warm glow stretched out from under the glass lampshade. There was no abnormal chill in the air, no sudden drop in temperature, no reason to drop to my knees to scan the immaculate hardwood floor for traces of black sand or other ritual components. Nate had made obvious attempts to make me comfortable and I smiled, appreciating his kindness.

I liked Nate, I had to admit. There had been a time when I honestly questioned if he was the reason behind Brynn's dark secrets and motives. But now, we finally understood each other and I could clearly see why my mother was so enamored with him.

"I don't need to tell you that going after Brynn that night was a measure beyond bravery. Nor do I need to mention that accepting her into your life now, after what you've been through, is an even more commendable act. Your history together has been long and trying, I've heard."

"When you're a child, everything is traumatic. I guess it takes a while to realize how silly it all is."

His eyes seemed to recall a suppressed memory for a moment, perhaps the real reason for Brynn's actions; the reason that would devastate a child enough to be willing to sell her soul.

"Teagan, you and I both know it lies deeper than that. Brynn's actions, especially of late, have been inexcusable."

"Well, as much as it would seem the more reasonable thing, I just can't seem to bring myself to hate her any longer."

"Ahh, she's grown on you?" he asked with a smile that seemed slightly forced for my sake.

"I wouldn't go that far. Yet."

Without any glossing over, or lengthy preamble, he handed me the thick leather journal. His brown eyes were serious, yet soft, in the firelight.

I looked up at him appreciatively, still afraid to see the secrets he'd kept logged in his coveted book. All I'd learned these past months, about guardians and heaven and even hell, had been discovered by someone other than myself. It was all within these pages. I only had to take it and finally come to terms with the fact that my burden could finally be lifted.

"Go on, take it."

I reached my hand out, then curled my fingers back. *What was wrong with me? What was I waiting for?* Then, deep breath inhaled and my fingers extended again, the smooth buttery feel of the leather was now in my hand. The book was softer than expected. After all these years, I expected it to feel cracked and dry, but instead it had become so worn with Nate's entries, it was just the opposite.

I looked up at him, still reluctant to open it without permission, but his gentle expression urged me on.

"Do you want me to leave you alone with it?"

"No." I said softly. Somehow I felt that would be the same as sneaking. The book still belonged to him and admittedly, his presence made me feel comfortable. He settled himself in the oversized chair behind his desk, giving me the quiet space needed and then, with a deep breath, I opened the cover. It was there, all of it.

Described in amazing detail, down to the dates, descriptions, everything. I still couldn't fully digest how Nate had become privy to all this information. How it all seemed to be here in complete, sequential order. No doubt, he dedicated a lot of time and energy gathering his information. I doubted the title *hobby* was even appropriate any more.

The date of my birth was the first entry logged, and I sighed to myself as my eyes followed the next date, which was the month and year of my father's disappearance. My schooling followed thereafter. He had even recorded the date Garreth registered at Carver High School and had recorded copies of our student schedules from this year and last. It was an entire collection of archives and honestly, it was pretty cool.

As I thumbed further, I found my father's birthdate was listed as well as my grandfather's, whom I had never met. A shiver of excitement ran through me.

Envelopes were pressed together containing various newspaper clippings of important events: my birth announcement, honor roll, even articles about the fire last spring had been neatly folded into an envelope and tucked into the spine. Another envelope, larger and manila in color, held copies of the medical records for both me and Garreth, a detailed description of our hospital stays, and strangely, Ryan's, as well.

Beneath the newer looking envelopes were a few that had yellowed with age. My finger gently opened the flap, pulling out a large, folded parchment. Carefully, I flattened it on my lap and read the names and dates of what I realized was Nate's own family tree. In utter amazement, I stole a peek toward the desk where he was sitting only to find he was purposely ignoring me, allowing me to discover and digest the journal on my own terms.

Brynn's essential information, of course, was also listed. A cloud of sadness washed over me as I read the names of her mother and still-born sister, followed by the dates of their births, as well as their deaths.

I noticed there was a black circle drawn around Brynn's name. It reminded me of the circle she cast in black sand—the circle that had been drawn against me intentionally, and a panicked feeling returned to my stomach as thoughts of Brynn alone with my mom down the hall surfaced. I looked up at Nate, bewildered.

"Sometimes doors aren't closed. They appear to be, but aren't."

"Are you saying Brynn could hurt me again?"

"I'm just saying you can't rid the world of evil completely, Teagan. You can stop it in its tracks for the moment, sometimes longer, but you can never take it away." The corner of his mouth lifted in a reassuring smile. "The world needs balance. You of all people know the importance of that. We need dark and light, good and evil, right and wrong. But what you discovered, Teagan, is that you have a special gift to block out what is dark, simply by not allowing it to overpower the light."

I fought the urge to roll my eyes at him and instead sighed deeply.

"Come." Nate beckoned with his hand for me to bring the journal across the room to him.

"Do you remember when I explained how the earth is a mirror image of heaven?" he asked, not bothering to wait for my answer. "If there are guardians to watch over earth, who do you suppose watches over the guardians?"

He rifled through the pages, not expecting me to answer but for me to speculate, until he came to the very last page, which was blank. But instead of concerning himself with the actual page, he instead slipped an envelope opener along the inside of the back cover. The stitching ripped open and a pocket was revealed. Nate slipped a finger inside the flap and pulled out a yellowed and fragile paper.

From where I stood, I saw that it had no words written on it, but instead the number eight was drawn in fine calligraphy across the entire page. Crossing over to the lamp with the reversed painting drawn on the inside of the glass shade, he pulled the thin chain, allowing the bulb to switch to a lower setting.

The pale light illuminated the glass and my eyes took in the dark lake, full of hands reaching up out of the water. I noticed the clouds were not clouds at all. They were wings, and an amazing number of angels reached down to the hands seeking them. In the dim light, he held the page up to the lamp and it mimicked the symbol in my hand. It wasn't an eight, but an incredible lemniscate and with the special help of the light, the document was revealed within the fibrous threads of the parchment.

Chapter Thirty-Six

My hand immediately sprung to my face in disbelief. "Is that my . . . ?"

"Your birth certificate, yes." I wanted to ask why it was hidden within a fragile piece of paper, but I couldn't seem to ask. "Of course, your mother has the legal document as well; I'm sure you've seen it. This particular copy is the most important entry I've collected to date. For reasons we've recently learned," he said with a grin.

When Nate realized I was at a loss for words, he picked up the pieces.

"You know Hadrian was your father's guardian?"

I nodded.

"You possess your own power, and it is much, much stronger than your father's ever was. Haven't you seen the signs?" Nate's voice was the softest I had ever heard it. "You are the light. A light sent from heaven to help cast aside darkness and fear. The light to see the good in all who have strayed from it. The light that guides the ones meant to watch over us."

I listened to him, taking it all in, confused.

"Think of all those who sought you out. Your human nature perceived it as taunting, as wishing to do you harm, and with the exception of the most recent, it has merely been souls looking for a light to help guide them. For now, you *have* helped Brynn."

In my hands I held the old paper with the incredible lemniscate drawn across it, my birth certificate protected within. I had always been guarded, always looked after, and it was funny that a piece of paper would be treated just as carefully. I traced the looping eight as I had often traced its replica in the palm of my hand.

"That paper is all the proof you need to finally realize you are more than you think yourself to be."

I nodded silently. His point was sinking in, but I wondered, "You said that doors can't really be closed. Then really, there isn't an end, is there?"

"There is no death for what is not human, but more appropriately, a change."

"I've heard that before," I whispered.

Hadrian.

Then suddenly, I realized.

He was safe.

My heart released all the guilt I had built up since returning from the tunnel. I had honestly feared the absolute worst, but to hear Nate repeat the very same words Hadrian had spoken to me once before erased all that. I knew, deep down in my heart that it was true.

"But as far as Lucifer is concerned, be wary of your thoughts," Nate warned. "You will meet him again if your mind is not closely guarded. Keep him at a great distance, for I fear he'll do you great harm if he gets the chance. You of all people know how close the realms are from one another."

I shivered at the thought of letting Brynn into my family. What if the day came when she would turn on me again? What about my mother's safety?

"What do you say we call it a day?" Nate closed the book and I realized he was guarding me, like Garreth and Hadrian had done all along. The words the journal contained weren't his secrets; they were mine, and they directly affected me.

I watched as he walked over to a painting I had never really paid attention to before. There had always been some sort of turmoil taking place in here for me to ever notice it during the few times I had been in this room. The large, heavy framed oil painting took up a good section of paneling. Something so large, only to be overlooked so often, made me wonder, how much did I really pay attention? Was I really seeing the bigger picture?

Standing up, I crossed the room to Nate's side. I placed my hands on top of his, realizing something I never thought of until now.

"We've all been caught up in the fact that for a very long time, Brynn has been without a mother, but I've grown up without a father . . . until now."

I flipped his hand over and held his mark up. "You're here because of me."

"I'll be proud to stand in and claim that role." He pulled me into a bear hug as the delicious smell of lemon bars made its way down the hallway to us and together we walked to the kitchen for a sweet end to our afternoon.

I could see the pattern starting here. A glimpse of the future. There were lemon bars and laughter, pizza, then a break for homework, followed by popcorn and a movie, and even more laughter.

Would I have pictured this a month ago? Not a chance. But here we were, the four of us, settling in as if we were a family. Brynn would jab my arm now and then, but not because she wanted to hurt me, but because she wanted my attention or to see if I thought something was just as funny as she did. At least for now.

My mother and Nate snuggled on the couch and I could see in both of their faces that this was right. That they had finally found the something that had been missing for a very long time, and deep down, I couldn't help smiling.

"Wow, ten-thirty already," my mom said as I stifled the second yawn of the night. "I nearly forgot these two have school tomorrow."

Again, it would have been awkward, except it wasn't. We said our goodbyes. My mom hugged Brynn, and I could swear I could hear the hardened shell of Brynn's exterior cracking. When they parted, she looked at me a little guilty.

"It's fine, Brynn. You can hug my mom."

She nodded and smiled back, still uneasy. I knew the hole was filling once again. She needed a mom and I was a big enough girl to learn it was alright to share mine. Brynn needed healing, and maybe that alone would be enough to keep her from being tempted by darkness's empty answers.

I pulled my coat onto my shoulders while my mother and Brynn walked on ahead to take one last peek at the kitchen, making sure the place was tidy enough to leave it for the night.

Nate leaned over to hug me goodbye.

"About the journal and everything, thanks. I mean it."

"I should be thanking you. It took me years to compile everything in that journal. I thought if I kept looking, I'd find the answer to why I had been given this mark. It was in front of me all along."

I hugged him back.

"Hey, this is good, right? You and I? We're getting that predictable hump of awkwardness out of the way when it comes to kids and stepparents."

"Yeah. Good thing I have my own car. We can hop over that one, too."

"Hmmm. What do we do when we're down to the last lemon bar?"

I gave him one of my serious looks. "Don't even go there." I was tired, but adrenaline was pumping through me. I knew there was one goodbye I needed to say, and I knew now was the right time to do it.

In the solitude of my room, I leaned back on my pillow and closed my eyes. I wasn't quite sure how to do this, except that calming myself and preparing my mind seemed to feel right. I began relaxing my muscles, then my limbs, starting at my feet and working upwards until every part of me felt blissfully peaceful, but alert.

My mind emptied of all the busy thoughts of the day, even though the entire conversation with Nate kept creeping in. I pushed it aside and concentrated. Within minutes I felt a floating sensation, as if my body was balanced on a cloud or laying in water. The motion rocked me slowly and gently, pressing me to ask for more.

I reached my mind out and felt the warmth of hers clasp around it.

I padded slowly over to my computer and pulled the chair out from my desk. Quietly, my fingers found the familiar keys and I opened my inbox, ready to begin the email I was finally able to bring myself to write. But the little icon in the corner caught my eye and everything tugged inside me all at once. I had an email.

Teagan,

All of the emails and the thoughts and the dreams . . . I've heard them from where I am. I didn't want them to go unanswered before I say goodbye. I'm glad Ryan has you for a friend. He sees in you what I've always known. Please tell him that I don't blame him for that night. Take care of my car, Tea. Play Pink now and then, just for me. And Tea, if the dreams stop for a while, don't worry about me, I'll always be here. My heart misses you.

Claire

My heart felt as if it was about to burst. I wouldn't forget Claire, but I was ready to let her go. Deep down I had been searching for a proper way to say goodbye, always remembering her and the friendship we shared, not just the tragic emptiness left behind. Somehow, this felt right.

I felt the air shift, growing wavy between us like heat on a dark surface. She was as thin as vapor, the sensation of her fading within me. In saying goodbye to Claire, I wondered if I was also severing another tie.

Hadrian.

So often he had been summoned to me when I emailed Claire, my thoughts filtering out to him. I had given him light in a world that had been too dark for too long and I comforted myself with the fact that somewhere he still existed and that this was how it was meant to be.

Chapter Thirty-Seven

The kiss on my forehead was like air. A whisper of breath, warm and light. My eyes opened to find they were staring into the finest of crystal blue, shining back at me.

"You were gone last night. I missed you."

Garreth was perched on his side, resting on his elbow, staring intently at me as if he hadn't seen me for a very long time.

"I know," I said reflectively. "There was a baking lesson at Brynn's. A history lesson in Nate's study and . . ." I paused, watching Garreth take it all in.

"What?"

He leaned over to me, taking my face in his one hand, and kissed me tenderly.

"I'm sorry," he whispered.

"Me too."

We shared a look between us, knowing all was forgiven.

"So, how does it feel? Knowing?"

"It feels good," I said with a smile.

Garreth leaned closer again, shifting his weight to pull me in to his chest.

"I love you, Teagan."

The sound of my mother rousing down the hall felt suddenly normal. I felt as if my world had moved out of place the last few weeks, then shifted back. Resuming itself.

"Guess that's my cue," Garreth whispered. We both knew my mom's routine well enough. She would walk sleepily down the hall, knock twice to make sure I wasn't snuggling back under the covers, then make her way to the shower. Garreth would be on his way out by then, fading into the beautiful, morning mist, only to return a short while later to take me to school.

The dresser drawer scraped shut through the wall. I could hear her feet padding their way toward my door. The predictable knock came.

"I'll see you in a few," my beautiful guardian whispered, but I stopped him, pressing my hand to his cheek.

"Things are different now. Stay."

His face registered surprise, but also contentment to go along with my train of thought.

"You're not acting like your usual self, you know," he said, with a teasing smile creeping slowly across his mouth.

"Apparently, I'm not an ordinary girl."

He settled back down, embracing me tightly, his lips on mine. From the other side of the hall, I could hear the water turn off in the shower. I was ready to say goodbye to the days of watching him leave, of watching him shimmer and fade. The last time he did that, he didn't return.

My mother learned enough about his world mirroring our own this week. Nothing unusual was left to make her head spin or leave questions dangling from her lips. There were no secrets anymore.

I sighed, reveling in the warmth of my angel's arms, with a sense of satisfaction. No more darkness, only light. I thought about the future: my mother's upcoming marriage, the strange fact that the girl who was once my greatest enemy would soon become my sister, that Nate was going to make a great dad – and Garreth. But in thinking to the future, I couldn't seem to let go of the past and all who had touched it. They flowed through my veins, forcing me to take stock of the wonder, the irony of how we were all connected.

Garreth, Hadrian, Ryan, Brynn, my mom, my father, Nate . . . and Claire. Eight lives that had touched my own. Eight.

I held them each within my heart, keeping them close and safe with the power of my thoughts. I was also careful to keep others guarded.

We have the power to entertain any thought we wish. To fully embrace them is another matter. Sometimes we get lost along the way, and sometimes we get lucky and find the answers.

I took Garreth's hand and opened the door. If we hurried, there would be just enough time to put a pot of coffee on for my mom before leaving for school. Pausing, I looked at the endless line of my lemniscate, how it traced and retraced its way across my hand, winding in and out, crossing back to the beginning. This was a new beginning, this world of light that was my own. It was beautiful and it was infinite.

Acknowledgments

It's time to thank some incredible people who mean the world to me!

First and foremost I owe a tremendous thank you to my family. To my husband Chris, for riding the rollercoaster with me and for listening to my incessant ramblings about writing, edits, plot ideas, and of course . . . books.

Thanks to my son Christian who always informed me when his friends mentioned my books and for sharing the love of YA fiction with me – to my daughter Megan for doing her best to understand when I hogged the computer and for squealing with delight whenever I revealed a new idea floating around my brain.

This would not be complete without my thanking the amazing people I've met along the way –

Tom Xander – your talent is truly a force to be reckoned with, an absolute gift. Thank you for devoting so much of your time to share my books with the world.

Lacey Williams – for your contagious enthusiasm! You are the countdown queen!

Michelle Flores – for not only being the first blogger to ever request an ARC of *Angel Star* but for also being a valuable friend. You're the best PITA anyone could have!

To the brilliant crafters of YA fiction who so graciously opened their arms and accepted me into their world – Cyn Balog, Christine Johnson, Liza Wiemer and my debut sisters Shelena Shorts, Shannon Delany, PQ Glisson and Jordan Deen.

To Kimberly Martin and Lori Coleman for design and editing, and making sure *Lemniscate* looked its best.

With absolute gratitude to my publisher, Lisa Paul, who uncannily shares the same vision as I do with this series and surprises me with text messages at random moments of the day to make sure I'm still alive.

Of course this would not be complete without saying thank you to everyone who has fallen in love with Garreth, Hadrian and Teagan – this one's for you!

9 780982 500583